D1011087

by LISA FIEDLER and anya WALLACH

Concept by Anya Wallach

PUBLISHED BY SLEEPING BEAR PRESS

Library of Congress Cataloging-in-Publication Data

Fiedler, Lisa, author.
Showstopper / written by Lisa Fiedler and Anya Wallach.
pages cm. -- (Stagestruck ; book 2)
Summary: "After the successful first performance by the Random Farm
Kids' Theater troupe, founder and director twelve-year-old Anya Wallach
turns her attention to their second show. But trouble rears its head
when their barn venue is jeopardized. Is the second show doomed before
they even start rehearsal?"--Provided by the publisher.
ISBN 978-1-58536-925-6 (hard cover) -- ISBN 978-1-58536-926-3 (paperback)
[1. Theater--Fiction. 2. Musicals--Fiction. 3. Friendship--Fiction. 4.
Community life--Fiction.] I. Wallach, Anya, author. II. Title.
PZ7.F457Sh 2015
[Fic]--dc23
2015007342

ISBN 978-1-58536-925-6 (case)
1 3 5 7 9 10 8 6 4 2

ISBN 978-1-58536-926-3
1 3 5 7 9 10 8 6 4 2

Cover design by Jeanine Henderson

Printed in the United States.

Sleeping Bear Press™

2395 South Huron Parkway, Suite 200
Ann Arbor, MI 48104

© 2015 Sleeping Bear Press
Visit us at sleepingbearpress.com

To Dolores Fiedler, who always listens
LISA

For my sister, Susan
ANYA

Hello again!

Doing something for the first time is in many ways easier than being able to follow up a success with a second act. When you accomplish something you've never done before—whether it's composing a song, learning a gymnastics pass, or making your school's basketball team—that first attempt you have trying to make it happen comes with the exhilaration of doing something new, and is filled with novelty and anticipation.

But then you want to continue the momentum. And that can be frustrating—and scary. Suddenly there are all these expectations. Can I do it again? How can I make it better? Will I have the stamina and patience to overcome obstacles?

In real life, the second Random Farms musical almost didn't happen (but I won't go into any more detail so as not to spoil the book!). Figuring out how to make modifications and adapt when there are complications are skills I developed quickly during my adventures running Random Farms. In live theater, you never know what will happen when the curtain goes up! I've had mics go out before an actor's big song, a costume piece (Belle's hoopskirt during *Beauty and the Beast*, to be exact!) fall off during a waltz, and a six-year-old Snow White who refused to go onstage right before the opening number.

Looking back, I think I learned more from the crash-and-burns than when everything went according to plan. I suppose it's those bumps in the road that make life interesting, right?

Now—on with the show . . .
Anya

CHAPTER

The day after the first Random Farms production was one of the most amazing days of my life.

Austin, Susan, and I had decided to give ourselves a much-needed day of relaxation, so we packed up our towels and sunglasses and went to the town pool, where we met up with Becky and Kenzie and a handful of other kids from the cast.

I was in heaven. All afternoon people kept congratulating us and asking about joining Random Farms. That wasn't even close to the reason I'd started the theater, of course, but I'd be lying if I said it wasn't kind of a cool perk.

I was proud of my cast and proud of myself. But a producer's work is never done, which meant it was time to start preparing for our second show. So after our lazy, relaxing Sunday, Austin and I arranged to meet up late

Monday afternoon at the coffee shop to plan.

I got there first, toting my laptop. I bought lemonade and a swirly iced cupcake, and picked a table. Three minutes later the bell on the door jangled, and Austin walked in. Thanks to our day at the pool, his nose and cheeks were a little bit sunburned.

I was surprised at how good Austin looked with that sunny glow. For some reason my heart sped up a bit.

He waved and went to the counter for an iced tea and a giant macadamia nut cookie. When he sat down, we got right to work.

"First things first," I said. "Finances."

Austin bit into the cookie and nodded. I opened my laptop and showed him the document my sister had titled *RF Financial.*

"So, according to Susan, we made a pretty decent profit." I pointed to the number at the bottom of the screen. "Not bad, right? We'll be able to cover our piano-tuning debt and still have plenty left over."

"Excellent," said Austin. "Add that to the next session's dues and potential ticket sales revenue following the second show, and we're definitely in good shape."

"Yes, we are," I said. "Moving on . . . Membership." I clicked a few times and showed him the two e-mails I'd received that morning. "Unfortunately, Sam isn't going to be able to be in the second show. He's got a lot of baseball stuff going on for the next few weeks. His team is heading for the pennant race or something like that."

Austin frowned. "That's kind of a bummer. Sam's a great kid. And a good actor."

"I know. I was pretty sad when I got the e-mail. But I understand baseball means a lot to him too." Then I indicated the last line of the e-mail.

" 'I'll def be back for the third show,' " Austin read aloud.

This resulted in a shiver of excitement along my spine. "Third show!" I repeated. "Sam's counting on there being a *third* show. That's encouraging."

Austin beamed. "Yeah, it is."

My excitement subsided as I clicked on the second e-mail. "Unfortunately, Sam's not the only one who's bowing out."

"Please say Sophia's decided to quit."

"We should be so lucky!" I rolled my eyes. "But no, as far as I know, Sophia the Diva will be back for the second show. It's Mia and Eddie who won't be able to do it. Family vacation. They'll be gone for two weeks."

"That's a *serious* bummer," grumbled Austin. "A double whammy! What are we gonna do without Mia's vocal talent and Eddie's comedic timing?"

"We'll just have to work around it," I said with more confidence than I actually felt. "And remember, a lot of our cast has improved a ton since we started."

"That's very true."

"And don't forget the new recruits. Those three kids we met at the pool yesterday—Nora, Brady, and Joey—they've got great potential. And Susan's been fielding tweets and texts all morning from kids wanting to sign up."

"So . . . you're saying our cast might actually increase?" Austin looked thoughtful. "That's going to be a huge factor in deciding on the next show. We're going to need something with lots of roles."

It was on the tip of my tongue to ask him if he thought he might be able to finish his big musical (the work in progress that had given me the idea to start the theater in the first place) in time to start rehearsing it a week from now. But after the theme song disaster, I'd learned my lesson about messing with a writer's creative flow. So instead I said: "*Annie!*"

Austin sipped his iced tea. "Annie who?"

"Not Annie who," I said, and laughed. "Annie the *musical.* Wouldn't it be awesome to do a full-length musical this time?"

Austin mulled it over. "Could be cool."

"Extremely cool!" I took a bite of my cupcake, being careful to avoid getting icing up my nose. "Ya see, I was thinking we could use my script from—"

I was interrupted by the jangling of the bell on the coffee shop door. Looking up, I saw a frantic Susan come skidding in.

"Anya! You have to come to the theater. Now!"

"Why? What's wrong?"

"I'm not really sure." Her eyes were wide, her face pale, and her tone was positively freaked. "All I know is that Mr. Healy's pickup is parked on the lawn. There are orange cones blocking off half the street, and the whole clubhouse is surrounded by fire trucks and police cruisers!"

Police cruisers? *Fire trucks?*

I looked at Austin. He looked at me.

We dropped our snacks and sprung up from our chairs. And we ran!

☆✦✧☆

The sprint from the coffee shop back to Random Farms Circle felt like a million miles. All I could think was that one of us had left something plugged in we shouldn't have, and the clubhouse had gone up in smoke.

Austin, Susan, and I were breathless when we barreled around the corner of our street. Red-and-blue lights flashed, and I could hear the crackling of walkie-talkie radios as the first responders communicated with one another.

What these first responders were actually responding *to*, I couldn't tell.

I gaped at the scene, feeling helpless. As I tried to make sense of what the policemen and firefighters were saying, I noticed a strange sound . . . a kind of squishing noise interspersed with muddy *splats*. Looking down, I saw that the clubhouse lawn, which had been so lush and pristine just the day before, was now a mucky swamp. The firefighters were having trouble walking across it; their heavy boots were being sucked into the wet grass.

"Why is the lawn so muddy?" Susan asked.

"Maybe from the fire hoses?" I guessed. But I didn't smell smoke, and there were no flames shooting out of the windows. That was an indescribable relief, but it didn't explain why the grass was so soggy.

We weren't the only people who'd come to find out what was going on. Several neighbors had turned out to watch the emergency personnel in action. A policeman was posted by the curb, making announcements over his cruiser's loudspeaker, cautioning the spectators to keep a safe distance.

When I saw Spencer, Maddie, and Jane watching from the other side of the street, I grabbed Susan's hand and ran to them.

"What happened?" I asked. "Was it a fire?"

"No," said Spencer. "I heard one of the policemen saying an underground water main burst a couple of hours ago."

It was only then I noticed the steady stream of muddy water rushing along the curb. Because I had headed out in the opposite direction on Random Farms Circle when I'd left for the coffee shop, I'd completely missed the commotion.

I let out a long grateful breath and smiled. "Well, that doesn't sound so bad. I mean, how hard can it be to fix one little busted pipe?"

"It's a bit more complicated than that," came a gruff voice from behind me.

I turned to see Mr. Healy, our neighborhood's grounds-keeper, approaching, a glum expression on his face. His denim work coveralls were soaked all the way up to his chest, and he was holding a heavy-duty flashlight.

"Just came from the clubhouse basement," Mr. Healy explained. "Flooded . . . Water's as high as the electrical panel, I'm afraid. Even deeper in some places."

"Uh-oh," said Austin. "That doesn't sound good."

I had to agree. I didn't know much about building mainte-nance, but I did know under any circumstances, water and electricity were never a good combination.

"Luckily, there wasn't much of anything stored down

there except for some old lumber the developer left behind back when he remodeled the barn."

I looked beyond Mr. Healy to where a group of workmen were lugging large sheets of plywood and a whole collection of two-by-fours out of the basement, dropping them for the time being in the empty field behind the clubhouse.

"Is there anything we can do about the flood?" I asked. I had a sudden crazy image of myself and my whole cast using giant pails to bail out the basement, like sailors on a sinking ship. I would absolutely do that if it would help. Something told me it wouldn't.

Now a police officer joined us. "Just got word from the chief," he informed Mr. Healy. "Department of public works says water service won't be functional for a while, and they've also asked for the power to be shut down for the foreseeable future."

Healy motioned with his flashlight to the houses closest to the clubhouse. "So these folks will be without running water and electricity for the rest of the day, maybe longer."

"And what about us?" asked Susan. "What about our theater?"

Mr. Healy shook his head. "In the clubhouse itself, you're lookin' at three weeks without power . . . at least."

"Three weeks?" Austin and I gasped in unison. That

was completely unacceptable. We would need access to the clubhouse *this weekend* in order to hold auditions.

"What if we promise not to turn on the lights?" I asked, desperate.

"The electricity is only part of the problem," Mr. Healy explained. "The basement is completely underwater. Could lead to mold issues. And remember, this is a very old barn. The building commissioner's worried about the stability of the foundation. Who knows what all that water'll do to those ancient support beams?"

Susan let out a snort. "Well, that would certainly give new meaning to a show 'bringing down the house,' wouldn't it?"

Austin shot her a heated look.

"Sorry," she mumbled. "Just trying to lighten the mood."

"Our props . . . ," I said, my heart plummeting to my feet, "and our costumes . . . they're all stored backstage. Are they going to get ruined?"

Mr. Healy shook his head. "Not likely. The water doesn't seem to be rising higher than the basement. Your stuff should be okay."

That, at least, was good news. Sort of.

One of the other policemen was motioning to the officer to return to the lawn. "You kids, promise me you won't go anywhere near that building," he said sternly. "If you need something from inside, we'll send a fireman in for it. No prop is more important than your safety. Understood?"

I nodded.

"Good," said Mr. Healy. "Because until we get the go-ahead from the city officials, the clubhouse theater is *off-limits*."

"We understand," said Austin in a grim voice. "Thank you, Mr. Healy."

I knew I should have thanked him too, but I just couldn't seem to get the words out. As I watched the groundskeeper head back to the theater through the line of police cars and fire trucks, I felt myself go numb.

Off-limits. Had a more disheartening word ever been spoken?

My cast members and I stood around a while longer, watching the fuss. Then Maddie and Jane hopped on their bikes, waving as they sped off to the Chappaqua Community Center to take a free origami workshop. Spencer left too; he was headed to Travis's house to shoot hoops in the driveway.

Must be nice to be carefree, I thought.

As Austin, Susan, and I made our way back to our house, the single bite of frosted cupcake I had eaten at the coffee shop sat like lead in my stomach.

We trudged into the family room and dropped ourselves into chairs. Through the big window overlooking the backyard, I could see the sun casting long shadows on the grass. When I was little, I always knew this particular shift in the light meant Dad would be home from work soon.

When I was little. Before I was an entrepreneur with big dreams and a flooded basement. I wondered if anything like this had ever happened to Andrew Lloyd Webber.

For a while we just sat there, sulking in silence. Austin was frowning and Susan looked heartsick. Personally, I was on the verge of tears! It was just so unfair. If we couldn't get back into that clubhouse, there wouldn't be a second show.

Finally Susan asked the question that was on all of our minds.

"Now what?"

"We find another venue," said Austin feebly.

Hah! As if *that* would be an easy thing to do. Finding the first one had been a challenge, to put it mildly. And then we'd done all that work, cleaning like mad and sprucing the place up, making it our own.

"Do you think if we explained to Mom and Dad about the flood, they'd let us have the rehearsals here?" Susan broached. "I mean, there's still a chance we'll be back in the theater by opening night. So it would only be two weeks of rehearsal."

"I suppose we could ask," I said. "But I doubt it." I felt a sudden irrational flash of anger toward my mother for being smart and industrious enough to run her own business out of our house. After all, that was the main reason we couldn't have the theater here at home—because it would interrupt Mom's work.

Then again I couldn't be too mad at her. . . . After all, I had wanted to do the exact same thing.

Susan's phone gave a little chirp, indicating a text message. She checked the screen.

"Don't suppose that's a message from the city officials telling us the floodwaters have miraculously subsided?" Austin joked.

"Nope," said Susan. "It's from Maddie. She sent me a selfie."

"Well, unless it's a picture of her signing a three-week lease on the Minskoff Theatre," I said, "I'm not interested."

Susan rolled her eyes. "Yeah, like they'd really bump *The Lion King* for us. But, hey, it's still a cute picture." She turned the phone so Austin and I could see the photo. "Look."

There were Maddie and Jane standing in the lobby of the Chappaqua Community Center, holding their little origami projects and smiling their heads off.

Then I spotted a small notice posted on the wall just over Maddie's shoulder, which (thanks to Susan's thumb and forefinger and the magic of iPhone technology) was now big enough for me to read.

"Summer rental prices," I read out loud.

"What are you talking about?" asked Susan.

"There's a sign on the wall outside the auditorium door," I said. "I forgot the CCC auditorium could be rented out."

"Hey, that's right," said Austin. "My mom was in a charity fashion show there last year."

"And my Brownie troop had our Fly-Up ceremony there back in first grade. Remember, Anya? There's a stage with curtains, and spotlights and a sound system and plush audience seating."

"That can be rented out," Austin said meaningfully.

I was utterly thrilled for the space of one second. Then I shrugged and let out a heavy sigh.

Susan gave me a sideways look. "Why don't you look more excited?"

"Because," I said, "it's a possible solution, but it's far from ideal."

"Perfectionist," said Susan.

I refused to take that as an insult.

"What does the sign say exactly?" Austin asked.

"It says, 'Chappaqua residents may rent this space for the following rates by signing up with the special events coordinator.'"

"We're Chappaqua residents!" Susan pointed out

unnecessarily.

"Thank you, Captain Obvious."

Austin used his own phone to log on to the CCC website and consult the fee schedule. "The prices are pretty reasonable," he pronounced. "We can afford this, as long as we're careful about our other spending."

"I guess," I said with a grimace. "But one of the best things about the clubhouse, other than the fact that it's ours, is that most of the cast can walk there. Only a few of the kids have to get a ride to rehearsal."

"Maybe we can work around that," said Susan, turning on the optimism. "You know the moms in this neighborhood are car pool geniuses!"

She was right, of course. I still wasn't crazy about the idea, but I also knew it was the only option we had at the moment.

So we switched from Austin's phone to my laptop, scanning the CCC website for more information. Unfortunately, that information included the following words: *Nonrefundable payment required in advance.*

"That's a problem," I said. "If we pay up front for the whole three-week session, and then the clubhouse *is* ready in time for rehearsals, we'll be out a fair amount of money."

Austin considered this. "Mr. Healy said we definitely couldn't get in for three weeks. This week we're off, so that means even though we'll be without the clubhouse theater for the first two weeks of the session, there's a chance we'll be in for tech week and the show."

"So . . . ," I said, puzzling it out, "you're saying we should pay up front for two weeks and hold rehearsals at the community center? And if the theater isn't ready by the end of the second week, we pay for the third week and have the show in the CCC auditorium?"

"Got a better idea?" asked Susan.

I didn't. "I guess this is what we're doing, then. Now we just have to hope it isn't already rented."

I reached for Susan's phone and began to punch in the number for the office of the special events coordinator.

I was about to hit the call button when the front door opened and my dad came striding in, holding two large plastic bags from our favorite Chinese takeout place. Judging from the serene smile on his face, I was pretty sure he'd come in from the west end of the street and hadn't seen the fire trucks.

"Girls!" he cried. "Guess who's taking your mother away next week on a long romantic second honeymoon to Paris?"

"Um . . . *you*, I hope," said Susan, raising an eyebrow.

Dad laughed.

And I put down the phone.

CHAPTER

It took some doing to convince Mom she should join Dad on his business trip to France.

To be perfectly accurate, it took some doing by *me* to convince her. Because the minute Dad announced his idea to take Mom out of town, an idea had begun to form in my head.

Austin went home, and Dad called Mom into the family room from her office. He told her he had a surprise, and it wasn't just the delicious dinner he'd picked up from Panda Pavilion. So Susan and I dashed to the kitchen for plates, and we all sat around the coffee table and listened to him explain while we passed out chopsticks and opened the cardboard containers.

Here was the situation: there was an important conference in Paris, Dad's law firm was sending him there to attend, and he had decided to bring Mom along as a sort of second honeymoon vacation. It was all very last-minute, because the partner who was originally slated to go, Henry Abernathy, had to opt out due to a gallstone attack.

"Somebody attacked Mr. Abernathy with stones?" Susan gasped, wide-eyed.

I had to laugh at that. Sometimes it was hard to remember that, for all her witty insight and advanced vocabulary, Susan was still only eleven years old. So Dad started to explain what gallstones were, but when he got to the word *bile*, Susan held up her hand to stop him.

"Never mind," she said.

Dad scooped more fried rice onto his plate and gave Mom his most charming grin. "Jennifer, we've been talking about going back to Paris for years. This is the perfect opportunity."

"I don't know. . . ." Mom shook her head. "It's such short notice."

"That's what makes it so exciting!" I said, eagerly reaching for an egg roll. "And romantic! I totally think you should go."

"But what about work?" Mom tapped her chopsticks on the table. "I suppose I *could* move some things around, reschedule a few appointments. . . ."

"Reschedule!" I said, gulping down a mouthful of tea. "Definitely reschedule."

"But what about you girls? Who'll watch—"

"Nana Adele and Papa Harold can stay with us!" I blurted out. "You know they're always saying they don't get to spend enough time with us. They'd be thrilled."

"Anya's right," said Dad, gallantly reaching over to take my mother's hand and kiss it. "So what do you say, *mon amour*? Will you let me carry you off to the city of lights to shower you with love and romance?"

Susan wrinkled her nose at this parental display of affection. "Eww! Speaking of *bile* . . ."

I gave my sister a sharp kick under the table to shut her up. This was going exactly as I had hoped, and I didn't want her to mess it up.

Mom crunched into a piece of crispy beef and sighed. "Okay," she said, smiling. "The answer is yes."

"I think you mean *oui*," quipped Susan.

I let out a shout of joy and sprung up from my seat. "I'll go get your suitcase out of the attic."

"No, you will not," said Mom, using her chopsticks to point me back into my chair. "You will sit down and finish your General Tso's chicken and tell me everything you've heard about this water-main break. I only know what Mrs. Quandt told me when she called earlier."

So I filled Mom in on what Mr. Healy had said about the

pipe bursting and the power being turned off at the far end of the street. I also mentioned a "water issue" in the basement of the clubhouse, but I didn't elaborate.

"We'll probably be okay for the show," I said, which, thanks to my careful use of the word *probably*, was not an entirely untruthful statement.

"What about auditions and rehearsals?" asked Dad, offering me a fortune cookie.

"Oh, I've got another place in mind," I replied vaguely. "Hey, did you know you can rent out the auditorium at the CCC for a very reasonable price?"

These, of course, were both completely factual statements, even if the two concepts were not as directly related to each other as I may have made them sound.

I could feel Susan looking at me out of the corner of her eye, but I didn't flinch. I just calmly cracked open my cookie and unfolded the fortune.

"What's it say?" asked Mom. "Something good, I hope."

"It says, 'You have a talent for getting what you want,' " I reported.

"Ain't that the truth," Susan said under her breath.

It took all my restraint to keep from kicking her again. I popped the cookie into my mouth and said nothing.

✩✩✩✩

"What was *that* all about?"

I looked up from where I was lying on my bed, flipping through my old *Annie* script, which I'd saved as a memento from when I'd been in a regional production of the play a few years back. I gave my sister an innocent look. "What do you mean?"

"You know what I mean!" she snapped. "You were pushing for Mom to go to Paris so hard, I was beginning to think you'd gone from being a theater producer to a travel agent!"

"Okay, fine," I said, closing the script. "I wanted Mom to go so we could have rehearsals here."

"I knew it! You lied to Mom and Dad!"

"No, I didn't," I said. "I told them we had another place in mind. I didn't specifically say what that place was."

"You said the community center."

I shook my head. "I *implied* the community center. They didn't press the issue, so I never actually had to tell them anything that wasn't true."

"Still pretty shady," Susan said, folding her arms in disgust. "Mom told us we couldn't have the play here."

"She told us we couldn't have the play here because it

would interrupt her work. But if she's in Paris, there'll be no work to interrupt, will there? So the way I see it, the rule about no play in the house no longer applies," I finished with a satisfied smile.

"I think that's what Dad would call a slipknot."

"Loophole," I corrected, my smile fading slightly. Because, technically, she was right. I *was* playing fast and loose with the rules. But it was such a lucky coincidence (for me, even if not for Mr. Abernathy) that the conference in Paris would be taking place during the same two weeks I would be without my clubhouse theater, I had managed to convince myself the universe was going out of its way to make things work in my favor.

And I couldn't very well say no to the universe, could I?

"There's a flaw in your plan, you know," said Susan, giving me a smug look. "You need to hold rehearsals here for two weeks. Mom and Dad are only going to be gone for one."

"I know that," I said. "But I'm counting on the fact that when they come back and they see how hard we've worked, and that we haven't destroyed the house, they'll let us continue for the second week until the clubhouse is ready."

"Seems risky."

That was because it *was* risky. But sometimes entrepreneurs have to face that sort of thing.

"Let's talk about *Annie*," I suggested, steering the subject away from loopholes and house rules. "I think we could put on a great production. Wouldn't Travis make a perfect FDR?"

"I guess," said Susan, sitting down on the bed. "What does Austin think about doing a full musical instead of another revue?"

I wasn't sure. His initial reaction had been that it would be cool, but we'd really only just started discussing the possibility when Susan had stormed into the coffee shop.

"Let's Skype him and see," I suggested, reaching for my laptop.

A moment later the cheerful *bing-bong* chimes of a Skype call filled the room, and Austin appeared on the screen.

"Hey, Anya," he said. "Susan. What's up?"

"We never got to finish discussing what play we wanted to do," I reminded him. "I say we go all out and put on *Annie*. I remember all the dance routines they taught me, and I have my script. We'll have to make copies of it for everyone, but how much can that set us back, right?"

"You'd be surprised," said Austin.

"What do you mean?"

"When I left your house, I did a little research."

"About what?" I asked.

"I started thinking like a writer," he explained. "And I

asked myself, 'How would *I* feel if just anybody who could get their hands on something I'd written used my work without my giving them the okay?' So I went online and checked it out and, sure enough, there are laws to prevent that kind of thing from happening. A play is considered 'intellectual property,' which means whoever wrote it owns it. Which is why it's illegal to put on a play if you don't license it from the owner."

"License?" said Susan. "You mean like to drive a car or own a dog?"

"Sort of," said Austin. "Basically, it means you have to get permission. You have to pay whoever owns the rights to the play in order to be allowed to perform it. It's kind of like renting."

I thought about this for a minute. "So if I were to use my script to put on *Annie* without getting the proper permission from the licensing people, it would be almost like stealing?"

"Not *almost* like stealing," said Austin. "*Exactly* like stealing. And there's more. The same goes for songs."

It took me a second to get the gist of what he was saying. When I did, my stomach knotted up. "Are you saying we were supposed to get permission to use every single song we performed in *Random Acts of Broadway*?"

On the computer screen, Austin nodded.

I'd had no idea! And from the guilty look on Austin's face, neither had he.

"Great," said Susan with a heavy sigh. "Mom and Dad are going to Paris, and *we're* going to jail!"

I had never felt so horrible about anything in my life. I had *stolen* the songs for the revue—unintentionally, of course—and my theater company had performed them without permission. And that was wrong.

So I wasn't a producer *or* a travel agent. I was a criminal.

"Here's the plan," I blurted out. "We get a license, and then we use the profits from our second show to settle up with the people or companies who own the songs we used in *Random Acts of Broadway*."

Austin nodded. "I agree. Honesty is the best policy."

"Oh yeah?" grumbled Susan. "And what are your thoughts on bankruptcy? Ya know, as a policy."

I let the comment slide. I knew it was going to be a difficult thing to do, but I also knew the only way I'd be able to sleep at night was if I paid back every last cent of what I owed.

"Okay," I said, shifting gears, "how much does it cost to license a play?"

"That kind of depends," said Austin. "There's a pretty specific formula that determines what you'll be charged for any given show."

"Sounds like math homework," grumbled Susan. "Bottom line . . . a lot or a little?"

"For *Annie*, a lot," Austin confirmed. "A real lot."

"I had a feeling," said Susan with a sigh.

"So that leaves us without a play," I said heavily.

"Maybe not," said Austin. "In my research I discovered lots of plays based on material in the public domain."

"Translation, please," said Susan.

"Nowadays all written work is copyrighted," said Austin patiently. "But the term *public domain* applies to work published before the current laws went into effect."

"So . . . old stuff?" I guessed.

Austin nodded. "Material in the public domain basically belongs to everyone. So if we wanted to, we could write our own play based on Shakespeare's *Romeo and Juliet*, or Anna Sewell's *Black Beauty*."

My eyes lit up. "We could?" *Black Beauty* was one of my favorite novels.

"We could if we had more than a week," Austin clarified. "It would take some time to adapt a story into a play, plus it would also require writing an entire score of original songs."

"Too bad about *Black Beauty*," Susan observed. "I would have given anything to see Sophia Ciancio play the back half of a horse!"

I shot Susan a look and she left the room, grumbling.

"So if we can't adapt something in time, how is this public domain stuff helpful?" I asked.

"Check your phone," said Austin.

On the screen he picked up his cell and hit a few buttons. In the next second, my phone dinged with a text: a link to a website called drama-o-rama.com.

"Drama-o-Rama?" I giggled. "I like it."

Drama-o-Rama was amazing. It had at least fifty kid-friendly (and, even more important, kid-*budget*-friendly) options to choose from. Straight plays, musicals, holiday specials—even one-acts. And for a relatively low price, a theater company like ours could rent scripts and scores.

"Austin, this is amazing!" I cried. "And cheap. We can afford to license one of these with pretty much our dues money alone."

"Now all we have to do is pick one," said Austin.

As my eyes scanned the available titles, I really had to hand it to the Drama-o-Rama writing staff. They sure knew how to spin things, and with a sense of humor. For example, *Totally Rad Riding Hood* was really just *Little Red Riding Hood* set in the radically tubular decade of the 1980s. And *Journey to the Center of the Mall* was clearly the story Jules Verne *would* have written if he'd understood the concept of the food court.

Also in our price range: *Dr. Jekyll Plays Hyde-and-Seek*; *Jane Airhead*; *Fence Painting for Dummies* (based on Mark Twain's Tom Sawyer); *Robin Hoodie* (comes with the sweatshirt); and *Tarzan Goes Ape: A Real Swingin' Show*.

There was even a musical called *The Princess and the Peanut*, designed to help boost awareness about the seriousness of food allergies. It included the song "I Want to Come Out of My Shell" and the dance number "My Kingdom for an EpiPen."

"Upbeat *and* educational," I observed.

"There's one based on *Ivanhoe*," said Austin hopefully.

"Ivan-*who*?" I asked.

"It's one of my favorite stories," Austin explained. "A classic by Sir Walter Scott about twelfth-century English knights. Do you think Maxie could get her hands on some suits of armor?"

"I doubt it," I said, quickly scanning the *Ivanhoe* blurb on the website. "And even if she could, it wouldn't work for us. It's a holiday show. See? *Ivan-ho-ho-ho: A Medieval Merry Christmas*. One of the songs is 'Silent Knight.'"

"Oh." Austin frowned. "I didn't read the whole description."

"No worries," I assured him. "There are plenty more."

I noticed a title based on another of my all-time favorite books, *The Secret Garden*, which the Drama-o-Rama drama-

27

tists had cleverly dubbed *The Garden Nobody Knew About.*

"Kind of girly," said Austin.

I knew what he meant. Frances Hodgson Burnett's novel is centered around a female character. I shrugged. "To be honest, I thought the same thing when you suggested *Ivanhoe.* I know there's plenty of romance in the story, but the main character is still a boy. Our goal is to find something that appeals to the broadest audience. It would be great if we found a play our cast members could be excited about, whatever their genders, with an equal number of girls' and boys' roles."

Of course, the gender breakdown of a show wasn't necessarily a deal breaker. We could easily have girls play boys or boys play girls if we had to. We'd tried that at our first audition, and it had worked out surprisingly well.

"Hey, what about *The Odyssey*?" Austin suggested.

I laughed, looking at the list. "I think you mean *The Odd-yssey.* Two Ds."

"The original material is the epic Greek poem by Homer," Austin explained. "It takes place in ancient times, and this solider—"

"Odysseus!"

"Right!"

"I know because we studied the poem a little in English

class," I said. "It's perfect. The subject matter is more appealing because the Greek goddesses are a lot more powerful than Ivanhoe's damsels in distress. There are plenty of roles that could be played by either boys or girls . . . like, monsters and mythical figures and animals . . ."

"So maybe we can cast Sophia as a horse's backside after all!"

I laughed. "Personally, I'd rather see her as one of Homer's classic monsters. The Cyclops, maybe, although knowing Sophia, she'd pitch a fit about only getting to wear *half* a pair of false eyelashes."

Austin was reading the information on *The Odd-yssey.* "This actually sounds perfect," he said. "It's got everything: adventure, suspense, romance, comedy." He looked at a sample of the sheet music. "The score is pretty simple. We won't have any trouble learning the songs."

I cleared my throat. "Speaking of songs . . . do you think we'll have our theme song in time for the show?"

Austin gave me a knowing look and we both blushed. The Great Theme Song Battle, as I'd come to call it in my head, hadn't been one of our shining moments. We'd moved past it, and I was pretty sure one day we'd both look back on the argument and laugh. But right now the embarrassment was still a little fresh . . . for both of us.

"I'll work on it," he said in a reasonable tone. "But I'm not making any promises."

"And I'm not making any demands."

So we officially agreed that Random Farms' second show was going to be *The Odd-yssey: An Epically Funny Musical.*

"The website says to allow three days for delivery," I said. "I'd better contact Drama-o-Rama right now if we want the material delivered in time for auditions next week."

"Sounds good," said Austin.

I logged off Skype and went downstairs to borrow a credit card.

CHAPTER

The next two days were all about preparing for the big trip and for Nana and Papa's extended stay.

On Tuesday Susan and I ran errands for Mom while she hunkered down in her office to wrap up current business and notify clients of her unexpected travel plans.

On Wednesday we got things ready for our grandparents' visit. Susan stayed home to tidy up the guest bedroom and bath, while I headed off to the market for groceries. My best friend, Becky, had a rare day off from her crazy sports schedule, so when she called that morning and asked if I could hang out, I invited her to come along.

Mom had given me a very specific grocery list and enough cash to stock the pantry until the next millennium. Becky pushed the cart while I scanned the shelves in search of the items on Mom's list.

"How's tennis going?" I asked, placing a box of oatmeal in the cart.

"Great," said Becky. "I'm ranked number one in my age division. I've got a tournament on Sunday afternoon. If I win, I go to the league championships."

"That's awesome," I said.

"Thanks." Becky was quiet for a moment. "So . . . how's Austin's original musical coming along?"

I shrugged, reaching for a jar of instant freeze-dried decaffeinated coffee. "I'm not sure. He hasn't mentioned it. I'm guessing he's still working on it, though."

As we wandered the aisles, we caught up on each other's lives: Becky told me about her new state-of-the-art tennis sneakers and her older brother's torn ACL, and I told her all about *The Odd-yssey*.

"I know Sophia is going to want to be Penelope," I predicted. "It's the female lead. I just can't picture her pulling it off. After all, Penelope is famous throughout history for being loyal and unselfish. And Sophia . . . isn't!"

Becky laughed.

I added low-sodium tomato juice, sugar-free butter-scotch hard candies, diet ginger ale, and all the ingredients for Nana's famous chicken potpie to the grocery cart.

Then I filled Becky in on our plan to move the rehearsals

to our house.

"Your parents are okay with that?" asked Becky.

"Well, they're not *not* okay with it," I said vaguely. "And it will only be for two weeks. Mr. Healy is pretty sure we'll be back in the clubhouse before tech week."

"When are auditions?"

"Saturday, bright and early," I said. "Swing by if you want."

Becky shook her head. "Can't. Tennis practice. But the match on Sunday is at the public courts in town. Maybe you and Austin can come watch."

I smiled. "Consider it done," I said.

We finished the shopping by picking out some frozen waffles, the makings for a Caesar salad, and baking ingredients, including chocolate chips and brown sugar (homemade cookies were a major perk of having doting grandparents visit). After we checked out, Becky gave me a huge hug and headed off to the pool for her diving lesson.

I collected my reusable shopping bags and hurried home.

It wasn't until I was dropping them on the kitchen counter and telling Susan, "*I* shopped. *You* put the groceries away," that I realized what Becky had said:

Maybe you and Austin can come watch.

Weird.

She'd invited me *and* Austin. What did that mean? That

she thought he and I were automatically doing that kind of thing together now, just because we were jointly running a theater program? Or did it mean she wanted Austin Weatherly to see how amazing she and her new cool sneakers were at tennis? It was hard to say for sure.

But I decided not to read too much into it.

I had a couple of grandparents and an epic play to prepare for, and both were going to require every bit of my attention.

☆☆☆☆

Drama-o-Rama promised "speedy and reliable shipping," and they didn't disappoint. On Thursday morning, the materials for *The Odd-yssey* arrived! A deliveryman in brown shorts hauled a hefty cardboard box up the front steps, and I actually got to sign for it. That felt pretty important. I'd never signed for anything before.

Susan helped me carry the box down to the basement, where we tore into it as if it were a treasure chest. The contents were as follows:

SCRIPTS (TWENTY TOTAL)
DIRECTOR'S GUIDE
PIANO VOCAL SCORE

SET/COSTUME/MAKEUP GUIDES
COSTUME/MAKEUP TUTORIAL CD
SOUND TRACK/SOUND EFFECTS CD
PERFORMANCE CD

It was basically a kit—Drama-o-Rama had provided the script and the music, as well as suggestions for things we'd need to gather on our own.

On the very bottom of the box was a large manila envelope containing a legal-looking document—the performance license.

"Wow," said Susan. "That's so official. We're big-time, now!"

I examined the CD cases and sighed. "Too bad we won't be able to use the sound track. I bet it sounds like a whole orchestra. Austin would love that."

"Maybe one of these days we'll be able to invest in a sound system for the clubhouse theater," said Susan.

"That would be awesome," I said. "But for now let's focus on getting this play in motion."

I picked up the script, flipping directly to the cast list, which I read from aloud: "Odysseus, Penelope, Telemachus, Poseidon . . ."

"Poseidon? Isn't he related to Ariel's dad in *The Little Mermaid*?"

"Yes," I said with a chuckle. "But way before that he was a pretty major figure in Greek mythology." I kept reading. "The Sirens, Athena, the Cyclops."

"The Cycle Ops? Who's he? The Greek god of training wheels?"

"Cyclops. Monster with one eye."

"Oh. Well, good luck to Maxie costuming *that*!"

I put down the script and glanced around the basement, realizing Maxie wasn't the only one who had her work cut out for her. This place was a disaster! My original plan for the theater (before we struck our deal with Dr. Ciancio to use the neighborhood clubhouse) was to clean up the cellar and use it as our meeting headquarters and rehearsal space. Looking around now, it was clear I'd underestimated just how much cleaning up it needed.

The whole place was dusty, musty, and cluttered. This was because none of us Wallachs ever came down here much, except to do laundry. The upside to this was that the ever-present springtime scent of fabric softener and dryer sheets helped mask the smell of mothballs and mildew.

"If we're going to hold rehearsals down here," I said, "we're going to have to spruce it up a bit. It totally needs to be organized, swept, and dusted."

Susan's response was a big sneeze. I took that to mean

she agreed with me.

"I'll go upstairs and get the broom and some rags. You can start moving those bins and boxes." I took the set list and the wardrobe suggestions out of the Drama-o-Rama box and handed them to my sister. "Go through these first to see if there's anything we can use for props and costumes."

Then I ran up to the kitchen and gathered the cleaning supplies. I was glad my mom was too busy packing to notice; she'd definitely get suspicious if Susan and I suddenly took it upon ourselves to clean the basement without being asked.

With a roll of paper towels tucked under my arm and a broom and dustpan in my hand, I clambered back down the stairs.

"Look!" said Susan, holding up a plastic pitchfork left over from the time Dad had dressed as a devil for Halloween. "All we have to do is spray-paint it. A little metallic gold, and Poseidon's got his trident."

"Excellent," I said. "Put it aside and we'll give it to Maxie on Saturday."

I dropped the cleaning stuff and helped Susan with the boxes. We found some fuzzy old bathroom throw rugs in various colors, which Susan thought Maxie might be able to turn into a Cyclops costume. Since the costume list called for a fair amount of togas, I was excited to find a whole pile of mismatched sheets.

"Wasn't there a pair of silver sandals mixed in with all the stuff Mrs. Quandt donated?" I asked.

"Yes," said Susan. "But I don't think Odysseus is exactly the sling-back type. I mean, Penelope, maybe, but only with her best Lilly Pulitzer toga."

"Stretch your imagination."

"I just imagined morphing some old bath mats into a mythological beast! How can I stretch my imagination any further than that?"

We had a big laugh when we found Dad's high-school yearbook (a mullet? Seriously, Dad?), and an even bigger one when we discovered Mom's prom dress.

"Taffeta?" quipped Susan. "More like 'laff-at-ya.' "

Where does she come up with this stuff? I thought.

"Let's hold off on the costume search for the moment," I suggested, grabbing the broom. "Maxie can hunt through these boxes over the weekend."

By the end of the day we'd managed to clear out a good-size space and eradicate most of the spiderwebs and dust bunnies. We'd also located an old portable CD player. Susan plugged it in while I removed the sound effects CD from its case.

" 'Track one,' " I read from the liner notes. " 'Wind.' "

Susan hit play, and the basement filled with the whooshing sound of 150-mile-per-hour gusts.

"Whoa," said Susan. "These Drama-o-Rama guys don't mess around, do they?"

Track two was "Rain." It began with a gentle pitter-patter sound but quickly upgraded to monsoon.

"I'm beginning to feel sorry for Odysseus," I said. "Vicious monsters and catastrophic weather conditions. Not exactly my idea of a fun trip."

Next we listened to "Groaning," which was followed by "Moaning," which was followed by "Howling," which was followed by "Goats."

"Goats?" said Susan.

"That's how Odysseus escapes from the Cyclops's cave," I explained. "By clinging to the underside of a goat."

"Clever," said Susan. Her face lit up. "Can we cast Sophia as the goat?"

When I frowned at her, she gave me an innocent look.

"Okay, so it was a b-*aaaaaah*-d idea."

I tried not to crack up. "Let's listen to the sound track."

I popped out the sound effects CD just as the "Battle Noises" track was about to start, and inserted the performance CD. Most of the songs had a strong Greek motif, featuring that plinky string sound I remembered from listening to my dad's original cast recording of *Zorba the Greek*. But there were other genres represented as well. When the goddess Athena, for example, appears to Penelope in a dream, she sings a disco number called "You Will Survive." And Penelope's rugged, toga-clad suitors perform a big Broadway-style dance number entitled "Everyone Goes!" And Telemachus, son to Penelope and Odysseus, sings a soulful country-western ballad called "My Young Greek Heart's in Ruins."

"Check out this one," said Susan, handing me a lyric sheet. "It's the Sirens' song."

I took the page and scanned the words to the song as Susan skipped to the next track on the CD. This selection was in the style of a 1960s Motown girl group, and the lyrics were hilarious:

Hey there, sailor boy in your big old ship,
Heading back to Ithaca on your homeward trip.
So you think you're gonna make it, gonna sail on past
'Cause you told your loyal crew to tie you up to the mast.
You made 'em plug their ears, yes, you flat-out insisted,
Because you know our Siren song no man has ever resisted.
We lure sailors to their doom, and we make no apology,
But that's the way it goes in Greek mythology!

I could already picture Madeline, Elle, and Jane singing this song, wearing sixties dresses and sporting matching bouffant hairdos, sky-blue eye shadow, and shimmering pale-pink lipstick. I described my vision to Susan.

"Perfect!" she cried. "Anya, this show is worth every penny we paid for it."

I was in total agreement.

CHAPTER

On Friday afternoon Nana and Papa arrived. And a few hours later Mom and Dad left for the airport. There were a few teary moments as we said bon voyage. It made me think of how Odysseus must have felt saying his farewells to Penelope and Telemachus as he set off to war. Of course, Mom and Dad were going to Paris, not Troy, and they weren't likely to encounter any mythical beasts or battles along the way. And I was pretty sure old Odysseus didn't have a set of matching luggage, like Mom did.

Still, she hugged Susan and me tighter than we'd ever been hugged before, and gave us all a final recap of the house rules, including a few I was sure would be obvious to a seasoned grandmother like Nana Adele: no chocolate chip cookies for breakfast, no staying up past midnight, no going outdoors without sufficient amounts of sunscreen. No purposely ingesting poison, no jumping off the roof with umbrellas, no running off to join the circus.

Okay, so maybe she didn't mention the last three, but that was kind of how it felt.

"Mom," Susan said with a huff, "we're going to be fine."

"I know, I know." Mom sniffled and hugged us again. "But remember . . . no cutting your own hair. And no tattoos."

We all laughed because we knew that last one was just a joke.

Luckily, Mom didn't say anything along the lines of "no play rehearsals at the house." I was still operating on the right side of the law—technically, at least.

When Mom and Dad were finally out the door, Susan and I enjoyed a terrific Caesar salad, courtesy of Nana, and Papa shared his butterscotch candies with us.

"This might turn out to be one of the best weeks of our lives," Susan observed, popping a third candy into her mouth.

"Let's hope so," I said.

✩✩✩✩

I was so excited to get started on *The Odd-yssey*, I barely slept at all. Knowing what I knew now about producing and directing and handling diva-size egos and guiding reluctant performers, I was sure this show would be as big a hit as our first one had been, if not bigger.

I just wished we had a home.

Because the clubhouse theater really had become exactly that: our home.

Odysseus would understand, I thought, rolling over in bed to see 6:45 a.m. displayed on my alarm clock. After all, that was what *The Odyssey* was all about—someone finding his way home.

I slipped out of bed, threw on a sweatshirt, and stepped into my sneakers. Then I tiptoed downstairs. Quietly, I opened the door, crept outside, and walked briskly toward the clubhouse. The sky was misty lilac, with a ribbon of deep pink along the treetops. I saw a few neighbors out for an early morning stroll and Mr. Davenport walking the family dog, a cocker spaniel named Patches.

I also saw Mackenzie Fleisch, which shocked me. She was dressed in a pair of running shorts and a baggy T-shirt, jogging along at a pretty good clip. Even her running was graceful. When she saw me, she stopped to catch her breath.

"Anya! I didn't know you were a runner."

"I'm not," I said. "I couldn't sleep, so I thought I'd walk over to have a look at the theater."

Kenzie smiled. "Well, I'm just about ready for my

cooldown. I'll come with you."

She fell into step beside me. "Do you run every day?" I asked, trying to imagine rolling out of bed on a summer morning to sprint around the neighborhood. Don't get me wrong. . . . I like exercise as much as the next girl, but I prefer to do it after the sun comes up. Especially during summer vacation, when sleeping in is practically mandatory for middle schoolers.

"Not usually," Kenzie replied. "But my mom was worried I might have put on a pound or two, so she thought I should get ahead of it. You know . . . more exercise, fewer carbohydrates."

I wasn't sure what to say to this. Mackenzie was as slender and fit as she'd always been as far as I could tell. If she'd gained a pound, I sure couldn't see it.

As we walked on, something occurred to me. "Hey, Kenz, can I ask you something?"

"Sure."

"Well, I know you've been dancing, like, forever, and you plan to become a professional ballerina someday, but . . . do you actually like it?" I shrugged. "I mean, do you love it?"

Mackenzie looked at me as if I'd just asked her if she believed the world was round. Then she laughed. "Nobody's really ever asked me that before," she admitted. "But yeah, of course I do."

I smiled. "I kind of figured," I said. "I guess I just wanted to be sure."

Mackenzie shrugged. "I mean, I don't always love the long drives into the city, or how snippy and competitive some of the other dancers can be. And I can really do without the sore muscles and bloody toes. But I'm really good at it. And it's fun to be good at something."

"Right," I said.

When we reached the clubhouse theater, I wasn't surprised to see the entire lawn was cordoned off with yellow caution tape. Even at this early hour there was a crew of workers on hand. I could see they'd set up a huge pump and were using it to siphon the water out of our basement. Men in neon-orange reflective vests were examining the storm drains; parts of the asphalt of Random Farms Circle had been torn up to give the engineers access to the broken pipe beneath the street.

It was a pretty gloomy scene.

Mr. Healy, who was talking to a man in a yellow hard hat on the front steps of the clubhouse, caught sight of me and waved. Then he gave me a shrug as though to say he still wasn't sure about the repair timeline.

I supposed a shrug was better than a negative shake of the head. A shrug meant there was still hope. So I waved back, and Kenzie and I left.

At the corner we went off in separate directions, saying we'd see each other at my house at ten. We both knew we'd rather be seeing each other at the clubhouse, but there was nothing to be done about that.

I had only taken a few steps when I heard Mackenzie call out, "Anya?"

I turned back. "Yes?"

"Do *you* think I've put on weight?"

I gave her what Mr. Healy hadn't given me: a definitive head shake. "No," I said firmly. "Not even an ounce."

Even in the pale morning light I could see how grateful she was to hear it.

The fact of the matter was that if anyone was carrying around some extra weight, it was me. Not physically, but emotionally. Thanks to the water-main disaster and the almost-lie I'd told my parents, I was beginning to feel as if the entire weight of the world were on my shoulders.

With a sigh, I headed home to get ready for the day.

☆✩✩✩

By 10:05, Susan had assembled the cast in our basement. From the top of the steps, I could already hear the joyful buzz of friendly conversations wafting up from below. My grandparents stopped me just as I was about to make my way down. They looked concerned.

"Anya, dear," Nana began, "Papa and I weren't expecting you to have so much company at one time. Isn't seventeen children an awful lot for a playdate?"

I gave her a nervous laugh. "Well, um, you see, Nana, it's not a playdate. It's the auditions for my theater. We're doing a second show, but the clubhouse is out of commission."

Papa's face lit up with pride. "You're doing another production! That's wonderful. You know, I've been a zealous theater fan since I saw Liza Minnelli make her debut at the Shubert Theater in New Haven, Connecticut, when I was just a young man."

"They know that, Harold," said Nana patiently. "You've told them the story a million times." She turned a worried look to Susan and me. "What's wrong with your clubhouse?"

I gave my grandparents a quick rundown on the water-main problem, and Mr. Healy's orders to keep out for the time being. "We'll be moving back to the clubhouse as soon as it's all repaired," I assured them. "And I promise we won't cause any trouble while we're here."

Before they could ask the obvious question—*did you clear this with your parents?*—I opened the cellar door. Susan dashed down the stairs, and I was hot on her heels.

When I reached the bottom step, the first person I spotted was Mackenzie, already stretching her dance muscles by using the back of an old dining room chair as a makeshift ballet barre. Sophia was admiring herself in my mom's antique cheval mirror (big surprise), blocking Gracie's view as she tried to pull her long black hair into a high ponytail. Susan was showing Maxie the bath mats and the other potential costumes and props we'd found while Deon handed out scripts that Jane, Elle, Spencer, Madeline, Teddy, and Travis were rifling through excitedly.

I was thrilled to see a handful of newcomers as well. These included three kids from my class at Chappaqua Middle School, who'd introduced themselves to Austin and me at the pool. They were Nora Standish, Brady Greenberg, and Joey Garcia. Joey had brought along his acoustic guitar, and he and Austin were hunkered down in the far corner, plinking out chords.

Another new recruit was Gina Mancuso, who would be going into sixth grade with Susan this year. Her dad was a well-known local builder, and everyone knew Gina had every intention of following in his footsteps. Rumor was last summer she and her three older sisters had built themselves a two-story tree house with real working windows and a

49

spiral staircase. I looked at her eager smile and could think of only one thing: master set designer.

Brittany Simpson was another of Susan's besties from Chappaqua Elementary. She had the reputation of being the best artist in the entire school. Visions of stunningly painted backdrops danced in my head, and I was sure Brittany and Gina would make a great team.

My arrival brought the happy chatter to an immediate hush as seventeen pairs of eyes (make that sixteen—Sophia continued to gaze adoringly at her own reflection in the mirror) turned to me.

"Hello, Random Farms!"

I was greeted with shouts of "Hi, Anya," and "Good morning, Madam Director," which made me smile.

Susan handed me an updated roster, to which she'd added the names and ages of our new cast members.

Just holding the list gave me a thrilling sense of possibility. So much talent!

But so little time.

"Let's get started," I announced. "Time for auditions!"

Just as we'd done with the auditions for the first show, the plan was for everyone to perform both a song and a dance combination today, and then memorize an acting piece to perform tomorrow.

CAST/CREW ROSTER: NAMES, AGES, ETC.

Mackenzie Fleisch: *Twelve; Dancer*

~~Sam Carpenter~~ (baseball conflict)

~~Mia Kim~~ (family vacation)

~~Eddie Kim~~ (see above)

Elle Tanner: *Ten*

Jane Bailey: *Eleven*

Spencer O'Day: *Eleven*

Nora Standish: *Twelve*

Joey García: *Twelve; Musician*

Brittany Simpson: *Twelve; Scenery*

Deon Becker: *Twelve; Tech genius*

Maxie Hernandez: *Eleven; Costumer*

Travis Coleman: *Ten; Dancer*

Gracie Demetrius: *Ten*

Madeline Walinski: *Eleven; Gum chewer*

Teddy Crawford: *Eleven; Professional actor*

Sophia Ciancio: *Twelve; Approach with caution*

Brady Greenberg: *Twelve*

Gina Mancuso: *Eleven; Set design*

After reading *The Odd-yssey* script, I was superexcited to see how my actors would interpret the various characters. For example, would Teddy read for the Cyclops in full-on comedy mode? If Spencer auditioned for the one-eyed monster, perhaps he might choose to play him more frightening. Maybe Gracie would decide to perform the goddess Athena monologue as a ditzy airhead, whereas Jane might give the lines a more sober, classical spin. To me, this was what made theater so fascinating—actors making interesting choices and bringing their own creative sparks to every role.

For the first show, Austin had preselected audition sides,

but today we were going to be a little daring and allow the actors to choose their own scenes.

I explained this to the cast. "Pick anything you like, from anywhere in the script, as long as it's at least a minute long. Girls can read boys' parts and vice versa. Feel free to add accents or quirks to your characters. If there's a role you think you're suited for, that's the dialogue you should read."

Sophia, who had finally pulled her attention away from her own face in the mirror, snatched up a script and flipped through the pages. "I can't decide if I want to read for Penelope or Athena. Penelope is such a romantic beauty, and the goddess is . . . well, a goddess. So I'm perfect for both."

Susan rolled her eyes. But before she could make a comment about goats, I hurried on.

"In addition to the dialogue, we're going to have you sing and also perform a dance combination."

"Mind if we watch?" came a deep voice from behind me.

I turned to see Papa and Nana standing at the bottom of the staircase. They both looked nervous.

"Um . . . everyone, start looking through the scripts," I said, then quickly went to join my grandparents. "What's wrong?"

Papa glanced over his shoulder at Nana, who gave him a worried look. Then he leaned toward me and whispered,

"Hate to be a party pooper, sweetheart, but your grand-mother is a bit concerned that . . . well, what with you young-sters being all alone down here, unchaperoned. You aren't planning a little game of . . . Spin the Bottle, are you?"

"*What?*" I was sure my cheeks had turned flaming red. Had Papa Harold just uttered the phrase *Spin the Bottle*? What planet was this? What universe was I in?

I shook my head hard and blurted, "No! Of course not!"

Papa patted my hand. "Good. As I say, I don't like to be a party pooper."

"There's no party to be pooped," I assured him. "This is an audition."

Papa looked at me closely, then nodded. "All right, then. We trust you, dear."

With that, they turned and headed back up the stairs. Just before the door closed, Nana's cheerful voice floated down to us. "Remember, children, there's a powder room in the front hall, in case anyone has to make."

Make?!

Seriously?

SERIOUSLY?

To my cast's credit, everyone managed to keep from cracking up. When I heard the basement door close, I let out a sigh of relief.

"Back to business," said Austin. "Everybody, take a few minutes to pick out your audition pieces. Then you can pair up with a scene partner if you need to."

"Last time we pulled names out of a hat to choose partners," Elle reminded him. "Should we do that again?"

Austin thought about it. "I think you can all partner up without a name draw," he said.

As our returning cast broke up into pairs and began searching their scripts, Austin turned to Joey, Nora, and Brady.

"Joey, are you planning on auditioning for an acting role, or are you strictly music?"

"I'm just here for the music this time," said Joey. "But maybe for the next show, I'll give acting a whirl."

"Well, I want to try everything," said Nora, beaming eagerly.

"I'm up for anything, too," said Brady, laughing. "I've never done any acting or singing or dancing before. Well, not in public anyway. But at home, in front of the mirror, I'm a star."

"I totally get that," said Sophia, giving him a flirty smile.

Again, Susan rolled her eyes.

I smiled and posed a similar question to Gina and Brittany. "I know you guys have major skills in art and building, but were you thinking about performing, too?"

Brittany raised her hand. "I'm a pretty good dancer. I could be in a musical number, but only if you need me. And I'd rather not have to say any lines. Mostly, I'd like to work on set design. Maybe help Maxie with the costumes."

The second she'd said, "I'd rather not have to say any lines," I felt a tingle shoot up my spine, and it immediately became my goal to get Brittany to want to say a line. Even just a single word! Because that had been one of the most gratifying rewards of the first show . . . seeing kids like Eddie Kim (who'd panicked at the thought of dancing) get up onstage and surprise himself with what he was able to do. I'd love to see the same thing happen with Brittany. I wouldn't push it, of course, but if the opportunity presented itself, I'd jump on it. I liked the idea of coaxing Brittany into taking a chance and having fun with acting.

"How about you, Gina?" I asked.

Gina shrugged. "Thanks, but I'm definitely a behind-the-scenes kind of girl, if that's okay."

"Perfectly okay," I said, waving Deon over. "D can tell you a little bit about the stage at the clubhouse theater, and you guys can look at the list of set suggestions that came with the play kit."

"Are there any suggestions about power tools?" Gina

asked, her eyes shining. "I really like working with power tools."

"Me too," Deon said, and laughed. "This is gonna be fun!"

I left them to their task and turned my attention back to Austin, who was showing *The Odd-yssey* sheet music to Joey, Nora, and Brady. The way things had worked out—with Gina and Brittany interested in being part of the stage crew and Joey opting for a spot in our "orchestra"—Nora and Brady would be the only new kids auditioning.

Since we didn't have a piano in the basement, I asked Joey if he'd mind accompanying the singers on his guitar.

"I'm kind of a beginner," he warned with a grin, "but I'll give it my best shot."

"That's all I ask," I said.

Then I invited Kenzie to kick things off by teaching everyone the audition dance routine. "Something simple," I advised. "Maybe a little portion of one we used in *Random Acts.* I know it'll take time away from memorizing your lines, so how about if you go last in the acting audition? This way you'll have a little longer to study."

"I'm cool with that," Mackenzie agreed, giving a cheerful nod.

I smiled because this felt like really good producing to me. During auditions for the first show, I probably would have been flustered by so many things going on at once. This time, though, I felt calm and well ahead of the curve.

For the next few minutes things at Random Farms were theatrically blissful. Kids were sitting cross-legged on top of the Ping-Pong table or flopped into our old beanbag chairs, silently reading their lines. Austin was helping Joey with the sheet music supplied by Drama-o-Rama, and Kenzie was breaking down a dance combination for Nora and Brady to perform. From where I stood, they seemed to be picking it up without much trouble.

And then . . .

I heard Nana's footsteps on the stairs.

I felt my heart drop to my toes. I had a horrifying image of her appearing with a dainty embroidered handkerchief, offering to wipe everyone's noses!

But when she reached the bottom of stairs, I saw this was much worse than a hanky situation. Nana was holding a laundry basket filled with dirty clothes.

Was she *nuts*?

I bolted across the basement to where my grandmother was preparing to toss clothes into the washing machine.

"What are you doing?" I asked, my voice rising with panic.

"I'm doing laundry, dear."

Well, I could see that. The problem was that she was doing laundry . . . *during auditions*. And what was even worse was that she was doing a load of *whites*, which didn't just mean sheets and towels. Whites meant *underwear*. OMG! What if she accidentally dropped a pair of my days-of-the-week undies in the middle of the floor for everyone to see?

"Nana!" I gasped. "Are you *trying* to ruin my life?"

She looked at me as if I'd lost my mind. "Anya, your mother's list of instructions clearly said Saturday is laundry day."

"But we're rehearsing!"

"Yes, I see." She smiled and tossed one of my dad's undershirts into the machine, followed by a few pairs of Susan's tennis socks. "That boy on the guitar appears to be a natural."

She really wasn't getting this. "Nana, I love you, but could you please leave? Now. I'm sorry," I added quickly. "I don't mean to be fresh. But I'm pretty sure Marianne Elliot never had to deal with her nana doing laundry while she was auditioning actors."

"Who is Marianne Elliott, dear? Is she in your class at school?"

"No, she's a major theatrical director. She directed *War Horse* on Broadway. . . ." I shook my head. "But that's not the point. Nana, can you please wait until after auditions to finish the laundry?"

"I'm sorry, honey. But if I don't get started on the whites now, I won't have time for the fine washables later." She closed the washing machine door and turned a dial on the control panel. "But here's the good news: I'm using the double-rinse cycle, so I won't be interrupting you again for at least fifty-five whole minutes."

"Great," I grumbled, watching her climb the stairs.

"Hey, stop that washer!"

I turned to see Susan making her way over from the far side of the basement. At least, I thought it was Susan; I couldn't see her face behind the enormous pile of old sheets she was carrying. Maxie was right beside her, lugging the bath mats.

"Stop the machine," Susan commanded again, her voice muffled through all that pima cotton.

"Why?"

"These old sheets are perfect for togas," said Maxie. "And Susan told me her idea for using the bath mats to make a Cyclops costume. Brilliant."

"But they're all gross and smelly," said Susan. "We can't use them unless we run them through the wash."

"Can't it wait?"

In response, my sister shoved the bundle of linens into my face. The stink of mildew told me she was right. The sooner we cleaned those sheets, the better.

I hit the stop button, opened the washer door, and watched as Susan and Maxie stuffed their haul of castoff bed linens and bathroom rugs in with the regular load. It was a tight fit. *Very* tight. We had to lean against the door to get it to click closed again.

"Maybe we should add more soap," Maxie suggested.

I opened the little compartment where the detergent went and poured in two more capfuls. Then I turned the dial to on and heard the *zzzzhhhsshhh*ing sound of churning water.

"That oughta do it," said Susan.

Oh, it did it, all right. . . .

It did it big-time!

CHAPTER

For the audition dance sequence, I chose sixteen counts of Travis's "Seize the Day" solo from our first show. Since Travis was such a superior dancer, Mackenzie altered the combination slightly to accommodate the fact that Brady had no dance experience.

First she walked everyone through the combination.

Pivot step, step ball change, kick, leap, step ball change.

After a couple of walk-throughs, Kenzie added the music, courtesy of my iPod speakers, which I'd propped on a shelf between Mom's long-forgotten Crock-Pot and Dad's high-school baseball trophies.

"Seize the Day" from *Newsies* filled the basement as my cast ran through the high-energy steps. I was enjoying their dancing so much, I was caught off guard when Brady stopped mid pas de bourrée and frowned.

"Um, Anya . . . I think there's a problem."

"With that last turn, you mean?" I gave him an encouraging smile. "Don't worry. You'll get it. You just have to shift your weight from—"

"No, *that's* not the problem." Brady pointed to the far side of the basement. "*That* is."

I turned in the direction he was pointing, as did everyone else, and my eyes nearly popped out of my head. The washer was overflowing! Water and soapsuds were gushing out around the edges of the door, and the whole machine was shaking and rocking and bouncing in place.

Talk about irony. . . . It actually looked like it was *dancing*!

"What do we do?" cried Susan.

"I don't know!"

But Austin had already sprinted across the basement to turn off the machine and switch the water line lever to off.

With a loud chug and a long hiss, the machine went still.

I stared in horror at the deluge of water and soap bubbles spreading across the floor. Travis's sneakers were already soaked through. Kids were hopping around, trying to avoid the flood by sidestepping or leaping over it, but since there was no longer a single dry inch of basement floor, they only succeeded in splashing through the giant puddle. It was like some nightmare version of that old Gene Kelly dance number

"Singin' in the Rain."

Susan was shaking her head in dismay. "Guess we should have used the extra-heavy cycle setting," she muttered.

I glared at her. "Ya think?"

Taking our cue from the rest of the cast, we splashed through the puddle and dashed up the steps.

☆✫✫✫

Upstairs, I explained everything to Nana and Papa: *Too many sheets . . . exploding washer . . . flooded basement.* They kept looking over my shoulder as actor after actor came squishing through the kitchen in sopping sneakers and squeaky flip-flops. I finished with a guilty shrug. "I'm really sorry."

"Oh, Anya," said Nana with a sigh. "I wish you had asked for my help."

"So do I," I admitted, feeling horrible. I couldn't believe Susan and I had destroyed not only our perfect rehearsal space, but Mom's top-of-the-line, energy-efficient front loader as well. And we'd made a lot of extra work for my grandparents.

"So, um"—I gave Nana a hopeful smile—"maybe we shouldn't mention this to Mom and Dad when they call. We don't want to worry them."

"Yeah," said Susan. "We don't want their second honeymoon to be a *washout.*"

Papa, who'd always gotten a kick out of Susan's sense of humor, laughed. Then he picked up the phone to call the plumber.

But Nana still looked very disappointed in me. And that made my heart hurt.

"I'm going out front to prune your mother's rosebushes," she said, slipping on a pair of gardening gloves. "Later on you'll have to help me empty the wet clothes from the washer and wring them out."

"Okay," I said. "Susan and I will do that. I promise." As she headed out the front door, I addressed my cast.

"I think we're going to have to do our singing auditions outside," I told them.

No one seemed to mind.

A few minutes later we were all seated on the back lawn in the shade of a big elm.

Joey, as it turned out, was a quick study when it came to music. Even though he'd never seen the sheet music before, he played the songs as if he'd been practicing for weeks.

After all the returning cast members had done their singing auditions (no surprises, except, I was happy to note, everyone was a lot more confident on this go-round), it was Brady's turn.

He gave us a rousing rendition of Cyclops's brooding solo, "In the Kingdom of the Blind, the One-Eyed Man Is King."

They say hindsight is twenty-twenty; that doesn't apply to me.
I've got one eye, and for me that's plenty—I see what I need to see.
Now it's never easy to make a decision
Without the benefit of peripheral vision. . . .

Brady's audition was terrifically entertaining; he really got into the giant monster character, and his baritone voice was perfect for the song.

"Wonder what size bath mat he wears," Susan whispered.

I giggled.

Then Nora performed one of Penelope's songs, the cute and upbeat "So Many Suitors, So Little Time."

Men in my kitchen, and men in my hall,
I'm in need of a way to get rid of them all.
I've told them a lie, now I have them believing
That I'll choose my next beau when I'm done with my weaving.

Nora also did a great job. With her height and strong voice projection, it occurred to me she might be exactly right for the role of Penelope.

"Wonderful," I said when she finished. "You should do the lines from that scene for your acting audition tomorrow. I'd like to see how it all comes together."

Nora beamed. "Okay. I will."

"You were both excellent," said Austin, offering Brady a high five. "Glad you decided to try out. And, Joey, thanks for handling the accompaniment. You did great."

"Thanks, dude," said Joey.

"See you all back here tomorrow morning," said Susan.

"Take your scripts. You can work on your scenes and monologues at home, and we'll meet back here tomorrow to finish the auditions. Ten o'clock. Don't be late."

"We won't," said Travis.

"Good luck with the flood," said Elle.

"See you tomorrow," said Spencer. "But just to be on the safe side, I think I'll bring my flippers."

"Hey!" Susan snapped, shooting him a look. "I'll handle the jokes around here, if you don't mind!" Then she grinned. "For the record, I would have gone with snorkel, but good effort."

Spencer laughed.

When they were gone, Austin, Susan, and I sat down on the porch steps. It seemed like only yesterday the three of us were having our first theater brainstorming session in this very spot. And now here we were, right back where we'd started . . .

both literally and figuratively. Because after today's washing machine disaster, and Nana's concerns about Spin the Bottle, it was pretty clear we would have to come up with a more appropriate place to hold rehearsals.

"It's karma," I said with a sigh. "I wasn't totally up-front with Mom and Dad, and the universe decided to punish me."

"Stupid universe," Susan muttered, dropping her chin in her hands.

"Kind of like the gods messing with Odysseus on his journey," Austin chuckled.

"You mean because Odysseus wants to get home to Ithaca, and we want to get home to the clubhouse theater?"

"Exactly," said Austin. "And as a writer, I like the symbolic connection. Life imitating art and all. But that doesn't help us with finding a better venue."

"Any ideas?" asked Susan.

"Just one," I said, standing and heading inside.

I returned a few seconds later, my pockets filled with ticket money, and started off down the walk.

Susan and Austin didn't ask me where I was going. They simply got up and followed me.

Because they knew as well as I did we had only one viable option.

The Chappaqua Community Center.

CHAPTER

After wandering the administrative hallways of the community center for a full fifteen minutes, we finally found the office of the special events coordinator, a Ms. Napolitano. Unfortunately, Ms. Napolitano happened to be away on vacation this week. She was taking a cruise.

Guess where.

The Greek Isles!

Austin the writer thought this was particularly fitting. Susan just rolled her eyes and blamed Zeus.

The problem was that Ms. Napolitano's temporary replacement, Mrs. Crandall, was not what you would call "well trained" in coordinating special events. Technically, she was a part-time employee whose usual job was to sit at the entrance to the indoor swimming pool, checking membership cards and reminding everyone to shower before getting in the water. I recognized her from when I took swimming lessons here back in second grade.

Mrs. Crandall was a very nice lady, but she was also a bit of a scatterbrain.

We explained to her that we wanted to rent the auditorium for the next two weeks, and if possible, we'd like to put a tentative hold on it for a third week.

This flustered her. "Are you sure you wouldn't rather just use the pool?" she asked. "I know how to handle that."

I politely assured her that unless we decided to reimagine *The Odd-yssey* as a water ballet, the pool simply would not do. We needed the auditorium.

It took Mrs. Crandall a while to find the rental forms in the ancient file cabinet, and accessing the events calendar on the computer nearly brought her to tears. Finally she was able to ascertain that the auditorium was, in fact, available for the dates we'd requested. She typed in the name of our organization and blocked off the next two weeks with a yellow highlight. The third week she highlighted in pink, which I supposed meant that it was not paid for yet and could change.

I gave Mrs. Crandall the cash, which she counted (twice). Then she handed over the forms.

"You can fill these out tonight and bring them back on Monday morning," she explained. "At least, I *think* that will be all right."

"Can we see the auditorium?" I asked.

"Oh." Her face fell. "Must you?"

"We must," said Susan.

"Very well." Mrs. Crandall opened a drawer and dug around until she found an enormous key ring.

"Right this way, children," she said, her massive collection of keys jangling.

We followed the substitute events coordinator out of the administration corridor, through the sports complex (where she cast a yearning glance at the pool entrance), and into the community center's main lobby, where three tall sets of doors led to the auditorium.

All locked.

Mrs. Crandall looked from the doors to the jangling key ring in her hand and appeared to be on the verge of quitting.

But sixteen keys and one call to the maintenance department later, we were in. The first thing I noticed was the size of the place. It was not as big as the auditorium at Chappaqua High (where we'd seen the drama club's performance of *Beauty and the Beast* last fall), but it was much bigger than our own clubhouse theater.

I pointed this out to Austin. "Think the size will intimidate our actors?" I asked. "If we're forced to do the show here, that is."

"I hope not," he said. "Let's check out the stage."

We left Mrs. Crandall at the back of the auditorium and hurried down the center aisle. I tried not to get overly excited about the real footlights and the complex arrangement of the rich, velvet curtains.

The sound system, according to Austin, was state-of-the art, as were the lights.

Susan scoped out the backstage area and pronounced it fantastic.

"Will this be suitable for your needs?" Mrs. Crandall asked.

"Very suitable," I said. "We'll see you first thing Monday morning."

Mrs. Crandall told me she'd leave the key at the front desk, which was a great relief to both of us.

☆⁂☆

At home, Susan and I pulled the unfinished load of laundry out of the washer so the plumber (who, according to Papa, was scheduled to arrive sometime between three and the next ice age) could repair the machine. We hauled the heavy, sopping sheets and bath mats outside, where we hung them over the railing of the back deck to drip.

"I'm starting to think maybe Austin had a point about that symbolic stuff," said Susan.

"What do you mean?"

"Well, in the play, one of the trials Odysseus faces is a violent storm at sea."

I raised an eyebrow. "Yeah . . . so?"

"So . . . Poseidon churns up the waters, and Odysseus's raft gets tossed and spun, dragged under by the waves."

"I know that. But what's so symbolic about it?"

"Anya"—Susan gave me a mischievous grin—"didn't you notice what brand washing machine we have?"

I shook my head. "No. What kind is it?"

Susan laughed. "It's a Whirlpool!"

☆⋆☆⋆☆

Since our rental agreement didn't officially go into effect until Monday morning, we were going to have to tough it out and hold Sunday's round of acting auditions in the backyard.

The cast arrived at ten o'clock. Travis was carrying a large shopping bag.

"Whatcha got there, Coleman?" Susan asked.

"You'll see," was Travis's cagey reply.

Then we got down to business.

We started with the monologues.

Sophia, not surprisingly, chose Penelope's romantic ode to her long-lost Odysseus. I had to admit, it was impressive. She even managed to dredge up a few tears. But she didn't show the same vulnerable quality I'd seen in Nora.

Teddy read for Poseidon and did a very admirable job. But since he was only eleven, his voice lacked the richness I was looking for. Austin agreed.

"He sounds too young to be a god," he whispered to me. "But I bet he'd make a great Telemachus."

Spencer's monologue was actually the prologue, or the opening lines, which set the scene for the upcoming action of the play. Members of the Greek chorus would perform these, and Spencer made the very cool choice of reading them like a circus ringmaster. It wasn't exactly how I'd envisioned the narrators; in my mind, these characters would be more along the lines of newscasters. But Spencer's interpretation showed great creativity.

Gracie capitalized on her comic strengths with Circe's monologue, and nailed it. She had everyone cracking up before she was even halfway through it.

"Excellent job on the monologues!" I said when she finished. "Let's move on to scenes."

The remaining actors quickly partnered up. Elle, Madeline, and Jane opted to read as a trio, doing the high-energy crazy Siren scene. I had pictured them in the roles the minute I'd seen the script, and they didn't disappoint. My only slight concern was whether Jane could handle the song. But her presentation had improved a lot since her first singing audition, and I knew she'd work hard.

Travis and Mackenzie had a surprise for us. They told us they were going to read a scene between Odysseus and the goddess Athena. Then they disappeared around the side of the house and returned thirty seconds later . . . in costume!

"OMG!" cried Susan.

Travis wore a long wig of black curls and bright red lipstick; Mackenzie was sporting a toga and a beard!

"Okay if we do a little gender-bending?" Mackenzie asked.

"Go for it!" I said.

And they did. They were *amazing*. Hilarious and over-the-top, but all within the context of their characters. Seeing the graceful Mackenzie trudge around and grumble like a weary warrior was incredible, and Travis . . . he *became* the goddess, portraying her as a total diva.

I glanced at Maxie, who seemed to wholeheartedly approve of their simple yet effective costuming choices.

"This could work," Austin whispered.

I nodded my agreement. But something was beginning to bother me. This script called for a lot more supporting roles than I'd originally realized. We would need at least four actors at any given time to play the Greek chorus, a handful for Penelope's suitors, and then there were Odysseus's men.

We might have to resort to the old stage convention of casting some of the kids in dual roles, which meant we'd be giving a single actor more than one part. This could be challenging even for seasoned thespians, since they'd need to rehearse and remember twice the dialogue, twice the blocking, and twice the number of songs and dances. While I was confident our actors were equal to the task, I suddenly found myself wondering if we could possibly enlist a few more kids to take part in this epic performance.

I'd talk about this idea with Austin later. Right now I wanted to enjoy Travis and Kenzie's scene.

When they were finished, the cast stood and applauded.

Travis laughed and tugged off his wig. "Phew! I don't know how you girls do it! This hair is hot! I'll take a buzz cut any day of the week."

That was the end of our acting auditions, but since it was still early, we decided we might as well work on some of the songs that involved the whole cast. Luckily, Joey had brought his guitar. I sent Susan inside to get our portable keyboard, and then we were ready to go.

Austin picked a scene that was actually a flashback, in which Odysseus explains how he managed to get inside the walls of Troy by hiding his army inside a giant hollow stallion. The title of the song: "Gotta See a Man About a Horse."

Everyone took a few minutes to go over the lyrics while Austin and Joey played around with the music. A few of the more experienced singers, like Sophia and Nora, began warming up their voices while others experimented with harmonies.

The cast's first attempt at "Gotta See a Man About a Horse" wasn't half bad. The tune was infectious, and the lyrics were clever and catchy. Austin incorporated a few of the keyboard's special rhythm effects, and enhanced the song even further by adding the reverb option. This, combined with Joey's acoustic guitar, made for a really great sound. It was almost as if we had an entire orchestra at our disposal!

And as for the singers—well, nobody held back! They sounded incredible, belting out the hilarious lyrics as if it were actually opening night.

They did an equally good job with "It's All Greek to Me," and I was proud of them. Last time, we'd auditioned with famous Broadway songs everyone already knew or at least had heard before. But everything about *The Odd-yssey* was brand-new and unfamiliar, which made it more of a challenge. And still, the cast had given it their all.

I suppose it didn't hurt that our musical's songs were "inspired" by well-known titles. But the melodies were altered and the lyrics were completely different. So I was pleased to see them catch on so quickly.

"That's all for today," I said when we finished our rousing rendition of "Some Gods Have All the Luck."

"Don't forget, tomorrow we'll be rehearsing at the community center," Austin reminded them. "If anyone has transportation issues, shoot Susan an e-mail or a text."

We all walked around to the front yard, where the cast said their good-byes and headed home. I was glad no one lingered, since I was anxious to start the casting process with Austin and to express my concerns about the size of the cast versus the number of roles we needed to fill. Plus, during the second verse of "Gotta See a Man," Becky texted me a picture of herself at the town tennis courts. This was followed by another text inviting me to come to her match later that afternoon. I responded with a simple:

I'LL B THERE.

As soon as Austin and I nailed down our cast, I'd go straight to Becky's match.

As I was waving good-bye to the actors, I got a third text

from my athletic bestie. Two words and an emoji:

BRING AUSTIN. ☺

I decided not to think too deeply on this addendum to her invitation. She knew we were holding auditions today, so she probably just figured Austin and I would be together anyway, so why not ask him along.

Right?

I tucked my phone into my pocket and joined Austin and Susan on the front porch. "Ready to cast the show?"

Austin held up a pad and pen. "Ready!"

CHAPTER

As Austin, Susan, and I sat on the front porch, I noticed what
a busy place Random Farms Circle was on a sunny afternoon.
I saw young mothers with strollers, kids on skateboards, and
older couples walking tiny fluffy dogs on leashes.

"I never realized how much foot traffic there is around
here," I said, an idea forming in the back of my brain. "I think
we can use that to our advantage, financially."

"How?" asked Susan.

"Well, one of the things on Mom's grocery list for Nana
was baking ingredients. Flour, shortening . . . chocolate chips."

"I'm listening . . .," said Austin.

"Broadway theaters sell refreshments, right? Well, what
if we held a pre-show bake sale? We can set up a table right
under the tree there. Look at all these people walking by! I
bet they'll be happy to buy a few cupcakes and cookies to

support the arts."

"I like it," said Susan. "Of course, I'm always up for anything that includes frosting."

"Let's do it," said Austin. "How about Tuesday, after rehearsal?"

I had Susan text the actors about my idea, and everyone responded that they thought it was a good one. Jane, Maddie, and Elle offered to bake brownies; Nora promised a batch of lemon bars. Spencer said his mother made the world's best Rice Krispies Treats. Gracie promised us a whole tray of baklava, and Gina informed us she had an uncle who owned an Italian bakery in Armonk; she'd see if she could get him to donate some pastries.

When Susan went inside to run the bake sale plan by Nana and Papa, Austin and I got down to business.

The Sirens were a no-brainer. Jane, Maddie, and Elle would play the mythical seductresses with a sassy sixties spin.

Casting the role of Penelope was equally simple. Austin and I agreed that Nora would be perfect.

"Sophia's gonna flip," Austin predicted.

"What else is new?" I sighed. "But Nora is the better choice. I was thinking we could give Sophia the role of Athena . . . until I saw Travis."

Austin grinned. "Yeah, he was excellent! I think he'll have

the audience in stitches."

So Travis was cast as Athena. We decided we'd have Maxie get him a better, less itchy wig and dress him in a flowing tuniclike gown with a golden belt. He'd be hilarious. In fact, he would bring down the house. I was laughing just thinking about him playing the beautiful and powerful goddess.

"And as long as we're thinking outside the box," said Austin, "what about Kenzie as Odysseus? She was terrific."

I considered this, then shook my head. "I'd rather see her play a character who does more dancing. It would be a shame not to showcase her talents."

"You're right," said Austin, tapping his pen against the pad. "Here's a thought. Sophia as Cyclops."

I laughed. "Oh, Susan will love that!"

"I know. But I'm not just suggesting this to get Sophia's goat."

"No pun intended," I joked, remembering that the Cyclops was, by trade, a goatherd. "But you make a good point. Sophia could really tackle the role. It would be a chance for her to prove she can actually act, and not always be the prima donna or the ingenue. She'll get to sing a solo, and she sure can't complain the role isn't big enough. I mean, the character's a giant. You can't get much bigger than that."

Austin wrote down Cyclops: Sophia Ciancio, then asked,

"What about Poseidon?"

"Brady!" I said without hesitation, picturing him holding our spray-painted trident and dressed in the gnarly swim trunks he'd been wearing at the pool the day we'd met him. "He can do it as a surfer dude, all laid-back and cool."

"Works for me." Austin wrote it down.

As we continued to cast the show, it became clear to Austin, as it had to me earlier, that we didn't have nearly enough actors for all the roles in this show.

"I guess we should have paid closer attention to the character breakdown before we chose this play," Austin said with a sigh.

"We're going to have to cast a lot of dual roles," I said. "The tricky part is going to be casting it so kids don't overlap with their own dual character."

"Right." Austin turned to a clean page on his pad, then opened the script and began to scan scene after scene, noting which character appeared in each one. Then he began to draw a diagram. To me, it looked like a sort of cross between a flow chart and a family tree.

"Look," he said. "Cyclops and Circe never appear onstage at the same time. So we can cast Sophia as both Cyclops *and* Circe, the goddess who turns Odysseus's men into pigs. And Telemachus and the six-headed monster Scylla don't overlap either. How about we cast Spencer as both of them?"

"He'll love it," I predicted. "Not sure how Maxie's gonna give him five additional noggins, but I'm sure she'll figure it out. Write it down."

It was like putting together some complex puzzle or solving a crazy brainteaser. We even had to take costume changes into consideration. We gave Brady the role of Antinous, the most arrogant of Penelope's suitors, and the part of Hermes (a speedy god sent by Athena to order Calypso to release Odysseus from her island, Ogygia) went to Elle. In addition to her chorus performance, Mackenzie would play Calypso. We'd have to juggle the members of the Greek chorus in a few scenes and switch out some of the suitors to play Odysseus's soldiers.

"But we're still going to have a hard time putting enough bodies onstage during the suitor scenes," Austin said. He gave me a sideways look. "Unless . . ."

"Unless what?"

"We actually recruit more bodies."

I sighed. "You mean bring in new kids?"

Austin nodded. "How else?"

"I thought of that," I said. "And I love the idea . . . in theory. But it's too late in the process to start adding new players. We'd have to put out feelers to bring kids in, then hold another round of auditions. I'm for growing the theater, but right now time is against us."

"I see what you mean."

I pondered the issue for a bit, and an idea struck me. "Why don't we just cast the kids we already have?"

"How?" Austin pointed to his flow chart. "We're already stretching everyone pretty thin as it is."

"I'm not talking about the actors. I'm talking about Maxie and Gina and Brittany and Deon. Even Susan."

"That's genius," said Austin. "I mean, they're already going to be around for every rehearsal. Why not let them get a little stage time!"

"Exactly," I said.

Then he lifted one eyebrow and smiled. "And what about you?"

"Me?"

He nodded.

It wasn't a completely wacky suggestion. After all, the whole idea to form this theater had been born of my two experiences *on* stage. In Hollywood, directors appeared in their own movies all the time. But I was pretty sure it was more unusual (if not downright unheard of) for Broadway directors to perform in their own plays.

"Maybe in the next show," I said at last. "I'm still trying to get a handle on this directing thing. And as for the rest of the crew, they'll have to be willing. I won't force them."

"What are you thinking for Susan?" asked Austin, his eyes twinkling.

"We both know there's really only one role that would do my sister justice. . . ."

I smiled and Austin smiled back as we announced in unison, "Zeus!"

I laughed. "The head honcho of all the gods! Who better?"

"Nobody," Austin agreed. "She's been rehearsing for this role her whole life!"

He wrote down Susan's name, chuckling.

"Okay," I said, folding my arms and giving him the same raised eyebrow look he'd given me. "What about you?"

"Wish I could but I can't."

"You can't? Give me one good reason why not."

"I'll give you eighty-eight good reasons why not," he said. "They're called piano keys. Think about it, Anya. If I'm onstage, where will the music come from? Joey can't do it all by himself."

As much as I would love to see Austin in a role, I couldn't argue with that logic.

Finally we had our cast list. It was a little strange to see

Deon's and Maxie's names there. I felt a momentary twinge of panic, wondering if they might not like the idea.

"They'll do it, won't they?" I asked. "You don't think they'll refuse, do you?"

"I don't think so," said Austin. "But like you said, we can't force them. The decision is really up to them. All we can do is offer them the parts. After that, the ball's in their court."

His choice of words had me jumping to my feet, as I suddenly remembered I had someplace to be.

"C'mon!" I cried, grabbing Austin's arm. "D and Maxie aren't the only ones who've got the ball in their court."

"What are you talking about?" he asked as I dragged him toward the garage to get my bike. "Where are we going?"

I told him.

And suddenly Austin was in an even bigger hurry to get there than I was.

CHAPTER

Austin and I got to the tennis courts just as Becky's match was about to begin. The Chappaqua Youth Tennis League was playing their biggest rival, Harrison Parks & Rec.

"Hey, Mezan!" I called, leaning my bicycle up against the fence and waving. Austin propped his bike next to mine and gave Becky a goofy grin.

"Hey!" Becky greeted us with a huge smile. "Glad you guys could make it."

"Wouldn't miss it," I said. "Cute skirt."

"Thanks." She turned to Austin. "Hi, Austin."

"Hi, Becky."

They just stood there grinning, and I noticed that for some reason, both of them suddenly looked like they were new to the planet. Like they'd never held a conversation with an actual human being before.

I was about to break the awkward silence when a whistle blew. The Chappaqua coach waved Becky over.

"I'm up," said Becky. "Talk to you after the match."

"Good luck," said Austin, flashing a terrific smile at Becky.

Becky's response was to do something I'd never heard her do before: giggle. For a minute I thought I was hearing things. In the nine and a half years Becky and I had been best friends, I'd heard her laugh, chuckle, crack up, and even snort soda out of her nose in a fit of hilarity. But I had never once heard her *giggle*. Becky was *not* the giggling type.

At least she didn't used to be.

But Austin looked like he thought that giggle was the best sound he'd ever heard in his life.

We found a place along the fence and settled in to watch. The opponent from Harrison was a blond girl wearing a blindingly white pleated tennis dress, and a terry cloth sweatband around her head.

Becky prepared to serve. She lobbed the ball upward, swung her arm down and around, and sent it flying like a little yellow missile.

"Perfect!" said Austin.

"Out!" yelled the line judge.

"What?" cried Austin, furious. "That was so in!"

It wasn't. It was out by a mile. Which was strange, because

Becky flubbing a serve was as unheard of as Becky giggling. When I saw her eyes dart over to where I was standing, it occurred to me that she was nervous. I couldn't imagine why, since I'd watched her play tennis a zillion times before, and my presence had never flustered her in the least.

It was a moment before I realized her eyes hadn't darted to me. . . . They'd darted to Austin.

Becky took a deep breath, positioned herself behind the line, and tried again.

I was amazed at how graceful she looked; her motions were every bit as choreographed and elegant as any dance steps I'd ever seen Mackenzie execute.

And this time the serve *was* perfect. It sailed at top speed, with a fierce, slightly downward trajectory, landing with a pop against the green-painted concrete. Blondie gave her best effort but missed the ball entirely.

Austin started applauding like mad.

I clapped too, although with slightly less excitement.

Becky served again; this time Blondie ran, pleats flapping, and managed to return it, but Becky was so fast and agile, she was practically a blur. Her backhand was like a lethal weapon. She scored.

Then she scored *again*. She simply could not miss. She seemed to have a knack for directing the ball to wherever her rival wasn't.

Becky won the first game, and they switched sides. She returned Blondie's first serve like a rocket, scoring easily.

This went on until Becky had thoroughly trounced her opponent. Austin and I cheered, laughing as the Harrison girl offered the winner the requisite good-sportsmanlike handshake while wearing the most unsportsmanlike expression on her face.

Becky came right over to us, grinning broadly. It was hard to tell whether she was smiling because of her victory . . . or because of Austin.

"I guess you were my good luck charm," she said.

"Happy to help," Austin replied.

I cleared my throat to remind them I was there. When I had their attention, I congratulated Becky, then took a step toward my bike. "We should get going. We've still got to put the finishing touches on the cast list," I said.

"Oh, that's right!" said Becky. "So what exactly is your play about?"

I gave her a quick synopsis of the epic adventure—the war, the suitors, the unpredictable nature of mythological bad guys.

"But the real depth of the play comes from Odysseus's longing to be back home," Austin concluded. "With the ones he loves."

I gave him an eye roll worthy of Susan's. "Don't you think you're overstating that love stuff a bit? I mean, the real meat of this play is the action."

"Action?" said Becky, pressing a towel daintily to her damp forehead. "What action?"

"Sword fights, daring escapes, hand-to-hand combat," Austin rattled off. "I just hope it turns out to be as exciting as the action I saw on that tennis court."

Becky beamed. "Thank you, Austin."

"I'm not kidding," he said enthusiastically. "I mean, if Odysseus could handle a spear the way you handled that tennis racquet, he'd be unstoppable." Suddenly his eyes lit up. "Hey. Maybe you could be our fight choreographer!"

"Your what?" said Becky.

I frowned. But not because it was a bad idea.

A fight choreographer is the person who designs and blocks all the physical violence in a play. Onstage scuffles may look improvised, but that was the genius of theater—every punch is planned, every attack rehearsed. This not only makes the fight scenes look better, it keeps the actors from getting unintentionally clobbered. I had to admit, after seeing Becky wield her racquet, what Austin was suggesting was actually brilliant. Her athleticism would translate perfectly into fight choreography, and it might just save us a few broken noses.

Becky would rock the job of fight coordinator.

So why did the idea bother me so much?

Maybe it had something to do with the way Austin was now offering to carry Becky's tennis bag for her. While I'd been mulling the suggestion over, he'd explained the job to Becky. Her eyes were now shining with interest.

"What do you think?" he was asking her. "We'd work the rehearsals around your sports schedule."

I laughed (it sounded more like a choke). "Well, *that's* not going to be easy," I said. "Becky's pretty booked up."

"Actually," said Becky, "my diving coach is away for a few weeks, so I won't be having lessons for a while. And since we just won this match, we won't have another one until the championship tournament, which is three weeks away. We'll still have to make time to practice, but if you guys can be flexible . . ."

"We can be totally flexible," Austin assured her.

I was actually gritting my teeth. Austin inviting Becky to be Skirmish Designer (or Brawl Coordinator, or First Assistant Director of War Craft or whatever title we ultimately decided to bestow upon her) without consulting me was simply unacceptable.

I was about to say we'd need to discuss the whole thing further, but then I noticed the expression on my best friend's face. She looked almost as thrilled as she'd been when she'd hit that final overhead smash to win her match. And I understood why: here at last was a chance for Becky and me to combine our passions and talents, to finally do something together and both shine at it. In the whole nine and a half years of our relationship that had never once happened.

I threw my arms around Becky and gave her a hug. "This is going to be amazing!" I said, and I meant it. "You don't need to come tomorrow or Tuesday, since we'll just be getting started and won't be ready to block the battle scenes yet. How about you report to work on Wednesday?"

"I'll be there!"

"Excellent," I said. "We'll messenger the script over to your house tonight."

"And by that," said Austin, crooking a grin, "she means we'll send Susan over on her bike to deliver it."

Becky laughed. "I'd better get back to the team," she said. "Anya, keep me in the loop, okay?"

I nodded.

As my best friend walked off, swinging her tennis racquet like a longsword, I told myself Austin had a great idea.

But what I knew deep down was that he had way more than just an idea.

What he had was . . . a crush!

⭐⭐⭐⭐

The whole bike ride home from the tennis courts, I was thinking about our expenses. We'd already shelled out a decent amount of money to license *The Odd-yssey*, not to mention we'd be settling up on the licensing fees from the first show later on. And on the chance that the clubhouse wouldn't be ready in time, we still might have to rent the community center for another week. So even if the bake sale was a huge success, we might still need a backup.

I decided it was time to shift into entrepreneurial mode.

As soon as we got back to my house, Austin and I sat down at my computer and Googled "Broadway money." What we found was a bunch of articles about investors. Simply put, investors were people who loaned money to a production. Not out of the goodness of their hearts, of course, but as a way of earning more money for themselves if the show becomes a hit.

So that was what I needed: investors. Otherwise known as backers. Aka angels.

"Angels?" said Susan when we explained it to her.

Austin nodded. "That's what they're called."

"Cute. So who ya gonna ask?"

Good question. I knew my parents would be happy to invest in my theater, but I just didn't want to ask them. I really liked the idea that this was a theater run entirely by kids; ideally that concept would apply to our backers as well.

As I was thinking this, I heard a loud rumbling sound.

"Are you playing the sound effects CD again?" I asked Susan.

"No, it's still in the basement." She went to the window and looked out. "It's Matt Witten. He's cutting the grass on his father's ride-on mower."

I'd forgotten Dad had hired Matt to mow the lawn this year. Matt was in eighth grade and lived two streets over from us. I remembered I'd had a crush on him last summer, because he smiled at me and let me cut in line for the diving board at the town pool. But I was over that now. Well, mostly.

I also recalled how, this past spring, Matt had sat at our kitchen table with my parents and haggled like a real pro before settling on a price for his landscaping services. As I understood it, he'd built up quite a client roster for himself by doing the same thing with Mackenzie Fleisch's parents, and the Quandts as well.

Susan turned away from the window, her eyes twinkling. "Matt must be making some big bucks this summer, huh?"

"You read my mind," I said, hopping up from my desk.

"Okay, listen. Go outside and invite Matt to come in for lemonade when he's finished cutting the grass. I want to have a financial meeting with him."

Susan nodded and dashed for the door. I told Austin what I was thinking, and he agreed it was a great idea. Then I asked him to wait for me in the kitchen, ran upstairs, and went straight to my closet. Because something told me that one of the first rules of business—just like in the theater—was looking the part.

CHAPTER

I changed into an outfit Mom bought me last year when I went into the city with Dad for Take Your Daughter to Work Day. At the time I'd felt like a total dork in the prissy trousers and boyish blazer. But today I was happy to have this power suit in the back of my closet. Paired with a crisp white blouse and my best flats, it made me look super professional.

I hurried into the kitchen and joined Austin just as Matt's ride-on mower sputtered to a stop by the front door. I took my place at the table.

Susan gave me a once-over as Matt rang the doorbell. "Hillary Clinton called. She wants her clothes back."

"Funny," I said, pouring three glasses of lemonade. "Go get the door. Then leave."

"What?"

"Susan, this is a financial meeting. I don't think having

my little sister hanging around is going to look very professional."

"Right," said Susan, eyeing Austin, then me. "Because everyone knows it's the twelve-year-olds who are running Wall Street."

She stomped off to answer the door.

I arranged *The Odd-yssey* script, the newspaper article about our theater from the *Chappaqua Chronicle*, and the program from *Random Acts of Broadway* on the table. Lastly I laid out our financial paperwork. All in all, I thought it made for a pretty compelling presentation. It said, *We are real; we are a success.*

A moment later Susan was leading Matt into the kitchen. He smelled faintly of grass clippings and gasoline, and there was a piece of mulch bark stuck in his hair. He also had his noise-canceling headphones resting around his neck, but I was not about to let any of this detract from the professional mood of this meeting.

Austin took a seat at the breakfast bar.

"Hey, Austin," said Matt. The boys fist-bumped, then Matt slipped into a chair and reached for a lemonade. "Hi, Anya. Haven't seen you at the pool much this summer."

"Hi, Matt. That's because I've been busy with my theater."

"Yeah." He took a long sip of lemonade. "I heard about

that. Things going well?"

"Yeah, it's a lot of fun. Well, except when the theater gets flooded and the lights go out and the washing machine explodes." I realized I was rambling, and I felt my cheeks turn pink. I wondered if that had anything to do with the fact that Matt Witten's eyes were bigger and browner and sparklier than I remembered. "Sorry. I guess it's kind of a long story."

Matt smiled. (Wow! His smile was a lot more dazzling than I remembered, too!) "I'd like to hear it sometime," he said.

"Well, I'd like to tell it to you sometime," I said with a grin.

When I glanced at Austin, I noticed he'd suddenly gone from looking happy about Matt's hearing our pitch to seeming a little . . . well . . . hostile. I had no idea why.

"What play are you doing this time?" Matt asked.

"It's called *The Odd-yssey: An Epically Funny Musical.*"

"As in the Homeric poem?" he asked.

I thought I heard Austin mutter, "Show-off," under his breath.

"Not exactly a Broadway classic," I admitted. "But it's going to be really entertaining."

"I'm sure it is," said Matt. "Theater originated with the ancient Greeks, after all. I did a term paper about it. Homer's poems were often performed."

Not to be outdone, Austin folded his arms across his

chest in a challenging pose. "Did you know the word *thespian* comes from the Greeks? Because the name of the man thought to be the first actor was—"

"Thespis," Matt supplied.

Austin frowned. "Right."

Okay, this conversation was getting weird. And so far it had nothing to do with asking Matt to invest, which was the whole point of the meeting.

"The ancient Greeks built huge outdoor amphitheaters where they performed their plays," Austin went on. "The seats were made of limestone, and they rose up, away from the stage, just like you see in modern theaters today. Even back then the Greeks understood how acoustics work."

"I did know that, actually," said Matt amicably. "In fact, as a visual aid for my English report, I built a detailed scale model of the theater at Delphi."

"Oh." Austin looked a little deflated, and I thought I heard him grumble something that sounded like "overachiever." I got the feeling he didn't mean it as a compliment.

"How's the landscaping business?" I asked, guiding the conversation toward our purpose for being there.

"It's a living," he joked. "I try to take advantage of my earning opportunities during the summer 'cause things always get a little crazy when I start my freestyle skiing training in the winter."

"Training," said Austin. "You mean, like lessons?"

"Not exactly." Matt hesitated, then explained in a modest tone, "My ski coach thinks I've got a shot at the Olympics in a few years."

"That's *fabulous*," I said, sounding like a starstruck schoolgirl. "The Olympics!"

"It's a long shot," Matt amended, with a shrug. "But who knows?"

"I'm writing a play," Austin blurted.

"Really?" Matt gave him a genuine smile. "That's awesome. Maybe I can read it sometime."

"Sure," Austin murmured under his breath. "Right after you win your Olympic gold medal or maybe while you're waiting to be awarded your Nobel Prize."

"Huh?" said Matt.

"He said, he'll send you a copy as soon as it's finished," I fibbed, giving Austin a sharp look.

"Well, I'm sure you guys didn't ask me in to talk about skiing," said Matt, taking another drink of lemonade. "So what's up? I'm guessing it has something to do with your next play?"

"Yes," I said. "I was wondering if you'd like to be my angel."

Matt nearly choked on his lemonade. "Your *what*?"

"My angel."

Was it my imagination or was Matt blushing a little? "Uh . . . is that anything like being your . . . um . . . *boyfriend*?"

Austin let out a loud snort of laughter.

"No!" I said quickly, wanting to crawl under the table and die of embarrassment. "I guess maybe the term *angel* does make it sound that way, but trust me, this has nothing to do with romance."

"Yeah," said Austin, eyeing my suit. "I'm pretty sure *that* conversation would require a very different outfit."

I shot him another look, and then I handed Matt the financial report Susan had prepared and printed out while I'd been changing into my business attire. It was an organized and sophisticated accounting of our expenses and profits with regard to the first show.

"Impressive," said Matt. "You guys pulled in some serious cash."

"We did," I conceded. "Unfortunately, in showbiz, you've got to spend money to make money."

Matt nodded knowingly. "Same thing in the landscaping business. I finagled myself a line of credit with Mr. Krause down at the filling station. Gotta keep that ride-on running, after all, and these headphones weren't cheap. I'm saving up to buy a mountain bike. I was hoping to have enough money by the middle of the summer, but it looks like I'm going to have to wait until fall."

"Which brings me back to the angel thing," I said with a smile. "Matt, what if I told you there was a way for you to make twice as much money in half the time?"

"Double my money?" His eyebrows lifted slightly. "I'm listening."

"In theater, *angel* is the term for someone who invests money in a show. Basically, it's a financial backer."

"Okay."

"So here's what I'm offering. You invest a certain amount of cash in our upcoming show. Cash we can use to buy props and costumes and for other incidentals that might come up. After the show, when we've gotten our ticket revenue, we'll pay you back . . . double what you invested."

Matt's eyes lit up. "You're kidding."

"Nope." I shook my head. "So for instance, using round numbers, let's say you invest two hundred dollars."

"Do you *have* two hundred dollars?" Austin asked skeptically.

Matt hesitated, then nodded.

"Perfect," I said. "So if you agree to be our angel, you'd entrust us with that two hundred for the next three weeks. You'll still be able to gas up your mower, thanks to Mr. Krause."

"Just curious," said Susan, popping into the kitchen to help herself to lemonade. "Is that line of credit only good for fuel, or can you use it at Krause's mini-mart for beef jerky and raspberry slushees?"

I gave Susan a glare. "Were you eavesdropping?"

"Not until he mentioned Krause's. You know I love slushees."

"That's not exactly pertinent at the moment," I said through my teeth.

"Slushees are always pertinent," she replied with a grin, flouncing back into the family room with her drink.

I turned back to Matt with a hopeful look. "You invest two hundred bucks and you get back four hundred. Without even lifting a finger."

He considered this carefully. "What if you don't make enough money to pay me back that much?"

I shook my head and pointed to the financial statement in front of him. "Not gonna happen."

"I admire your confidence," he said. "But c'mon, Anya. As a businesswoman, you know there's no such thing as a sure bet. Anything can happen."

I couldn't argue with that, not when there was a busted water main less than half a mile away to prove his point.

"Okay, well, how about this? We guarantee at the very

least you'll get your original investment back . . . with ten percent interest. That's a twenty-dollar profit."

"You can buy a lot of slushees with twenty bucks!" Susan called from the family room.

Matt was quiet for a long moment, and I was sure we'd lost him. Then he picked up the program and examined it thoughtfully.

"Mr. Davenport cuts his own grass," he said at last.

I frowned, not getting the connection. "So?"

"You've seen his yard, right?"

"Of course. It's the biggest, fanciest one in the whole neighborhood."

Matt nodded, and an expression of yearning flickered across his face. "Two and a quarter acres, perennial beds, boxwood hedges, and all those climbing roses on the pergola."

"Yeah, yeah," said Austin impatiently. "Davenport's got a green thumb. We get it. What's that got to do with us?"

"The Davenports' son, Kyle, used to do all the yard work, but he's backpacking through Europe this summer."

"Good for Kyle," snapped Austin. "Again, how is that relevant?"

Matt grinned, flipping through the program. "I could make a real bundle if I had Mr. Davenport as a client."

He was leading up to something; I just wasn't sure what.

I leaned back in my chair, folded my arms, and cocked my head. "So why don't you?" I asked. "Have him as a client, I mean."

"Because I'm a horticulturist, not a door-to-door salesman. Between your yard and the Fleisches' and the Quandts', I don't have time to ring every doorbell in the neighborhood, trying to drum up more business. My mom offered to call the ladies in her book club to see if any of them needed a landscaper, but that felt way too babyish."

I smiled because I knew exactly what he meant. It was, after all, the whole reason I'd set up this meeting with him, instead of just asking my parents for a loan.

"But if I could find a way to do some effective advertising," Matt continued, "aimed directly at the residents of the Random Farms neighborhood . . . well, I might get Mr. Davenport's attention. And Mrs. Campbell's, too. Have you seen the amount of dandelions in her yard?"

"So you're saying you want to advertise in our theater program?" I said, finally catching on.

"A full-page ad," he said, "at no cost to me. And it should identify me as an investor. I think your audience would like knowing they're doing business with a patron of the arts."

Okay, A) I loved that Matt Witten could use the term *patron of the arts* in conversation, and B) it was a brilliant idea and a great compromise! Even if, by some horrible chance, *The Odd-yssey* didn't earn enough to double Matt's investment, he'd still benefit from the free advertising. And it was very professional; Broadway Playbills (like the one I'd sold to Sophia Ciancio) always featured advertisements.

"Done!" I said, reaching out to shake Matt's hand, and not even minding the smudges of black engine grease on his knuckles. Then I grabbed a pen and quickly jotted down the specifics of our deal: the doubling of his two-hundred-dollar investment, or (should things go terribly wrong) the return of it in full with 10 percent interest, and a full-page ad to be designed by him.

Matt looked over the document, then signed the paper as Susan returned to put her empty glass into the sink.

"So I'm an angel?" said Matt, meeting my eyes and giving me another great smile.

"Oh, I can practically see the wings sprouting between your shoulder blades as we speak," deadpanned Susan. "Just watch out you don't damage your halo when you put those headphones back on."

I was glad she said something because, for some reason, with Matt smiling at me like that, I was having trouble finding my voice.

"We'll scan it and e-mail a copy to you right away," Austin

promised Matt, then downed the rest of his lemonade.

"You know," said Matt, "there's that huge overgrown meadow behind the old clubhouse."

"Clubhouse *theater*," I corrected. "But what about the meadow?"

"I've asked Healy a few times if he'd pay me to clean it up. But he says there's no point in landscaping property nobody sees or uses." He gave me a grin. "Think you could use your influence to get him to reconsider?"

"Mr. Healy's got his hands full at the moment, with the water-main break and all," I reminded him. "But if the opportunity arises, I'll definitely mention it."

"Thanks, Anya."

"Thank you, Matt."

Austin practically leaped off his barstool to show Matt to the door. When he came back, I poured him a second lemonade and we raised our glasses in a toast.

"To angels!" I said.

"Even the ones who smell like grass and gasoline," Austin added.

I giggled as we downed our drinks.

CHAPTER

On Monday morning the cast of Random Farms met on the steps of the Chappaqua Community Center.

Papa Harold drove Susan and me, as well as Spencer, Jane, and Maddie. The rest of the kids either biked or arranged car pools. Gracie's big brother, Nick, drove her along with Elle and Travis. I had to laugh because Nick was driving the car he used to deliver pizzas for their uncle George's restaurant. It had the words **DEMETRIUS'S PIZZA** emblazoned on the side, and even a loudspeaker attached to the roof!

I was surprised when Nick got out of the car and opened the trunk. He carefully removed something wrapped in a soft flannel cloth, which he handed to Gracie. Then he got back into the car and drove off.

"Does anyone else smell pepperoni?" Susan asked as Elle and Travis joined us.

"That's what happens when you get dropped off by the pizza guy." Elle sighed, sniffing her sleeve.

"Could be worse," Travis noted. "We could smell like anchovies."

"Look on the bright side," said Susan. "You'll never be late for rehearsal."

"Why not?" asked Elle, scraping a glop of old mozzarella from the bottom of her sneaker.

"Because Demetrius's promises to deliver in thirty minutes or less!"

"What's that?" I asked Gracie when she reached the steps.

Gracie unveiled the object. "It was a gift to my dad from his papou," she explained.

I looked at the peculiar-looking item cradled in Gracie's arms. It was clearly some sort of musical instrument, like a guitar without a neck, or a baby harp.

"It's beautiful," said Susan. "What's it called?"

"A kithara," said Gracie. "When I told my dad we were doing a version of *The Odyssey*, he thought we might be able to use it."

"Wow," said Austin. "Awesome lyre."

Gracie scowled. "Who are you calling a liar? It *is* a kithara and my dad *did* say we could use it!"

"I'm not calling you a liar, Gracie," Austin clarified. "I'm calling the kithara a lyre. It's just another name for it." He reached out for the instrument. "May I?"

Gracie handed him the instrument. Austin plinked the strings. It made a sound similar to a guitar, but a little deeper and pluckier.

"Can I try?" asked Joey.

"Wait!" I said. "That thing didn't, like, belong to Apollo or anything, right? It's not some priceless artifact unearthed from a Greek ruin, is it?"

Gracie giggled. "It's just a good reproduction. Not a toy, but not an archeological treasure, either."

"Well, be careful anyway," I advised Joey as Austin presented the lyre to him.

Joey examined it. He was at first tripped up by the fact that this instrument had ten strings, whereas his acoustic guitar had only six. But after a minute or so, he was strumming away like an old pro. "I bet I can find a lyre tutorial on YouTube," he said. "Gracie, mind if I take this home for practice?"

"That's fine," said Gracie.

"All right, everyone," I said. "Let's go inside."

We entered the lobby, and I went to the desk to retrieve the key Mrs. Crandall had left for us. Seconds later we were stepping into the theater.

For a moment everyone just stared in silence.

"This is great!" cried Jane at last.

"It's huge," said Maddie.

"Check out all the lights!" Deon said breathlessly, eyeing the spots and canisters suspended above the stage. "And there's a sound system! Man, I think I've died and gone to heaven."

I wasn't sure I liked the idea of my cast being so awed by this place. I understood that the plush auditorium seating and the gorgeous velvet curtain were impressive. But that didn't make me feel any better about their excitement level. I didn't want them to love it more than they loved the clubhouse theater.

"It'll do for now," Austin pronounced diplomatically. "We'll make the best of it, and get back home just as soon as we can."

"Like Odysseus," said Teddy.

I smiled, pleased he'd made the same connection Austin and I had.

"Speaking of Odysseus," said Maddie, "are you guys going to post the cast list?"

"Yes," I said, turning to Susan. "Did you remember to bring the Scotch tape?"

As soon as I stuck the list to the wall, I stepped back to avoid being trampled by my eager and curious cast. Susan, of course, hung back with Austin and me, as did Maxie, Brittany, Gina, Deon, and Joey.

There were a lot of happy squeals and no small amount of confused whispers. After a minute or so, Travis turned away from the list, wearing a puzzled expression.

"This says I'm playing Athena *and* a pig. What's up with that?"

"That's kind of a surprise," I explained. "We're casting everyone in dual roles."

"Why?" asked Jane.

"Simple math," said Teddy, who seemed pleased with having been given the title role of Odysseus. "There are more parts than actors."

"They do it on Broadway all the time," I explained. "In *Peter Pan*, for example, the parts of Captain Hook and Mr. Darling are traditionally played by the same actor. But in that case, it has less to do with math than making an artistic statement."

"It's going to make for some challenging costume changes," Maxie observed.

Elle giggled. "Max, that's not the only challenge you're going to be dealing with."

"Whaddya mean?"

Elle pointed to the cast list. "Says here you're in the show.

You're a member of Odysseus's army *and* you're one of Penelope's suitors."

Maxie blinked. "I am? But I didn't audition."

"Neither did Deon or Brittany or the rest of the crew," Spencer pointed out. "But they've all got parts, too."

"We do?" said Gina, sounding nervous.

"You don't have a speaking part," I assured her. "Unless you want to try that. But at this point, all you have to do is help fill up the stage. Same for the rest of you."

Maxie and Deon both looked relieved. Gina's fellow set designer, Brittany, was clearly excited about the chance to perform, and Joey—typical mellow musician that he was—didn't seem to care one way or the other.

"Susan, look!" cried Elle. "Your name's up here, too."

Susan marched toward the cast list. Upon seeing her name beside the character Zeus, she let out a little yelp. "Me? Play Zeus?"

"You'll be perfect," Austin assured her.

"Zeus is a boy," Susan reminded us.

"And Athena's a girl," said Travis with a shrug. "But I'm playing her."

Susan looked from one grinning face to another, finally meeting my hopeful gaze.

"Will you do it?" I asked.

Susan bit her lip. "I'm not sure about this, Anya. I mean, Zeus is so bossy and intimidating, and really smart and super important. Do you really think I can handle it?"

"Handle it?" I said, approaching her and draping an arm around her shoulders. "You were *born* for it!"

Susan laughed. "I guess you're right. Okay, I'm in."

As the other actors congratulated Susan, I snuck a look at Sophia.

Just as I'd expected, she was fuming over being cast as the Cyclops, as opposed to the female love interest, Penelope.

"This is a joke," she said, leveling a look at me. "You can't possibly be serious about me playing a *monster*!"

"Why not?" said Susan. "It's not like it's a stretch."

"Susan," I said sharply. "That was uncalled for."

Then I drummed up my resolve and turned to Sophia, forcing what I hoped was a calm and reasonable expression. "As the director," I began, "I don't owe anyone any explanations. But I want you to understand that Austin and I chose to give you this role because we're confident you'll do a wonderful job with it."

"I don't want to do a wonderful job as a monster," Sophia spat. "I want to do a wonderful job as a Siren, or as the lovely and loyal wife of the hero."

"Did you notice you've also been given the role of Circe?"

Elle pointed out hastily. "According to the script, she's a real femme fatale. I'm not sure what that means exactly, but it sure sounds like you."

"It means Circe's a beautiful goddess who is irresistible to men," Maxie piped up. "I bet I can make you a stunning toga with marabou-feather trim."

I knew they were trying to be helpful. But I refused to *beg* Sophia to play Cyclops. She should be happy to have such a terrific role. She should recognize that a real actor would welcome the opportunity to show she could play any kind of character. Even a one-eyed one.

"Look, Sophia," I said before anyone else could start offering bribes. "I would like to see you step outside your comfort zone and play Cyclops, but if you aren't willing to do it, I won't force you. I can give the role to"—I hesitated only a second—"to Austin."

"Me?" said Austin.

I gave him a wink, indicating he should just play along.

"Oh, right," he blurted. "Me! I'll play Cyclops."

"But if you refuse to play Cyclops, I'm going to have to rethink your playing Circe." I shrugged, then repeated something I'd heard my mother say to Susan more than once. "I'm not going to reward bad behavior."

Sophia was staring at me with such a heated look on her

face, I half expected fire to start shooting out of her ears. After a long, excruciating moment, she opened her mouth to speak.

I braced myself.

"Anya?"

"Yes?"

"Do you think I should play the Cyclops more as a big nasty bully, or kind of as a bumbling dolt? I can do either, you know. I'm *that* good."

I smiled, trying not to look as relieved as I felt. "That's up to you," I said easily.

"I think either choice works," she went on confidently. "In fact, I bet I could figure out a way to combine them. I mean, he's a monster, so he'll have to be all gruff and growly. But he's also sort of a dimwit, which will give me a chance to show off my comedic talents."

"Yes," I said. "That's exactly what Austin and I were thinking when we cast you in that role."

"Now . . .," she said, her smile widening. "About Circe . . . well, that should be simple for me. After all, the first two words in her character description are *beautiful* and *powerful*. Talk about a role not being a stretch."

I forced a smile but didn't comment. This superior, self-satisfied attitude of hers was obnoxious, but since it was easier to deal with than a full-on conniption, I decided to quit while I was ahead.

"All right, people," I said, clapping my hands for their attention. "Let's start with a read-through. Everybody, to the stage."

Obediently, they all shuffled down the carpeted aisle of the theater and up the steps on either side of the stage. Scripts in hand, they sat down, assembling themselves into a wide oval on the black-painted floor.

"Susan—highlighters," said Austin.

Susan made her way around the oval, handing out the neon-colored markers to everyone who had a speaking part.

"What are these for?" asked Maddie.

"To highlight your lines for easy reference," I said. "When you're done, we're going to start with a read-through."

"What's a read-through?" asked Brady.

"Exactly what it sounds like," I said. "You just sit where you are and read through the script, without any blocking or moving around."

Susan finished distributing the markers. As the actors began the task of highlighting their lines, she gave me a puzzled look.

"What's wrong?" I asked.

"When I put the highlighters in my backpack this morning,

I counted out just the right amount," she said. "One per kid."

"And?"

She held up a neon-green marker and frowned. "There's one left over."

"Maybe you miscounted," said Austin.

Susan rolled her eyes. "Have we met? I'm an organizational genius. I don't miscount."

"Wait," I said. "You weren't expecting to need a marker yourself because you didn't know you'd be highlighting lines of your own."

"Right," said Susan. "Which means I'd be one *short*."

"Well, even organizational geniuses make mistakes once in a while," I said.

I waited for the actors to finish coloring their lines. When they were done, there was a rustle of pages as they turned back to the first scene, then a hush fell over the theater. They were waiting for me to start them off. I glanced at Austin, who was standing beside me with our script—the director's copy—open in front of him.

I smiled and took a deep breath. "Whenever you're ready."

Silence.

I tried again. "Start when it feels right," I said a little louder, in case the acoustics of this huge space were working against me.

Still, nothing.

Heads began to swivel. Kids frowned and whispered.

I turned to Austin. "What's the first line?" I asked.

He consulted the script. "'Reporting live from ancient Greece . . .'"

"Who says it?"

"Greek Chorus Number One."

I closed my eyes, picturing the cast list:

Greek Chorus Number One: *Mackenzie*

It was then I realized . . .

Mackenzie was nowhere to be seen!

"Maybe she had one of those super-special, last-minute New York City dance classes her mother's always springing on her," Susan guessed.

Austin shook his head. "I doubt it. She would have texted one of us."

"No, she wouldn't," Maxie corrected. "Her mom took her phone away last week. She said it was distracting her from dancing."

I reached into my pocket for my own cell. "I'll call her house phone," I said. "Maybe she overslept or something."

"Actors, start looking at your lines," said Susan. Then she grinned, raised her arms in the air, and said in a deep, booming voice, "Useless mortals, I command thee to start looking at your lines by order of Zeus, father of the gods."

I gave her a look. "That's gonna get old fast," I warned as

the phone rang once, twice . . .

"Hello?" came Kenzie's mother's voice through the speaker.

"Hi, Mrs. Fleisch, this is Anya Wallach."

"Good morning, Anya."

"Is Mackenzie there?"

"No, she's not. She's gone out for a run."

"Oh. Well, when she gets back, would you tell her—"

"She won't be home until much later today. She's meeting her friend Annabelle for a Pilates class at the yoga studio in town, then Annabelle's mother is driving them to the Dance Warehouse to buy some new tights and leotards. Then they're going to the dance studio to take an extra ballet class."

"Oh." I blinked. "Wait. She's . . . what?"

An impatient sigh came through the phone. "Can I take a message?"

"Um, sure. Can you please just tell her—"

At that moment the auditorium doors burst open and a very sweaty Mackenzie entered the auditorium.

"She's here!" cried Elle.

"Never mind, Mrs. Fleisch," I said awkwardly. "Thanks anyway. Didn't mean to bother you."

I heard a click as Mrs. Fleisch hung up on her end.

"Sorry I'm late," Mackenzie said, coming down the aisle, her cheeks brightly flushed, her chest heaving.

I gaped at her as she took off her backpack and fumbled in it for a bottled water. "You ran here? All the way from Random Farms?"

Mackenzie took a long sip and nodded.

"What about Pilates?" I asked, still confused. "And the Dance Warehouse?"

A strange expression flickered over Kenzie's face; she didn't seem to know how to answer me, and for a minute I was afraid she was suffering from heatstroke.

"Your mom said you were meeting dance friends," I prompted.

"She did?" Mackenzie took another gulp from the bottle. "Weird. She must be thinking of the weekend. I told her I had plans to do that on Saturday." She laughed. "She's been so busy lately, trying to get me an audition with one of the New York ballet companies, she can't keep anything straight. I'll call her when we take a break and clear things up."

I frowned. That did not sound like Mrs. Fleisch; Mrs. Fleisch could tell you the time and location of every dance class Mackenzie had ever taken since the age of three, plus the name of every instructor she'd ever studied under, and the current height, weight, and body mass index of every ballerina in the tri-state area who might constitute a threat to Mackenzie's standing as one of the best dancers in her age group. I knew because I'd heard her do it. But I wasn't about to point this out to Mackenzie, who was now digging her script out of her backpack.

"You're Greek Chorus Number One," I said, "which means you've got the first line. You're also playing the nymph Calypso. And maybe Charybdis, if Maxie can figure out how to costume a character who is technically just a wild and watery vortex of evil."

"Cool." Mackenzie made her way to the stage and took a seat between Nora and Maddie.

I looked at Austin.

He looked at me. "Was that weird?"

"Very," I said. I decided to let it go this time, but from now on I was going to have to be more of a stickler about punctuality.

"Let's go, Director!" Susan bellowed. "We're wasting time, and we don't have a minute to spare. This is an epic, not a one-act, ya know!"

"Ya think maybe this 'leader of the gods' thing is starting to go to her head?" Austin asked with a grin.

"God or no god," I said, heading toward the stage. "She's still my little sister, which means I have absolutely no problem wrestling her to the ground and sitting on her head. I've done it before and I'll do it again."

Austin smiled. "Good to know."

We took our seats in the front row and the read-through began.

☆⭐☆☆

Despite Kenzie's tardiness, we wound up having a great read-through. The script was well written and totally hilarious! There were a few references that went right over our heads, but thank heavens for Wi-Fi. Every time we came across some mythological-themed joke or pun we didn't quite understand, Susan would look it up on her iPhone.

"I am Zeus!" she hollered. "Knower of all things!" Then she held up her smartphone and sang out praises to its power. "I hold in the palm of my godly hand the very secrets of the universe! I hold an iPhone. . . . I hold the world!"

"Wow," said Teddy, who had a few TV commercials on his professional résumé. "Great slogan! You should call Apple's marketing department and see about becoming their spokesperson."

"Spokes-*god*!" Susan corrected with a haughty snarl.

"Enough," I said. "Now put the phone down and go get the sheet music." Then I added, "Please," because A) it was polite, and B) I didn't want her to get any crazy ideas about smiting me with a lightning bolt.

After our read-through we spent the rest of the day working on the songs.

At Austin's suggestion, we started with the ensemble numbers. After a bit of experimentation, Joey managed to get some great sounds out of the lyre, and once again Austin got creative with the prerecorded rhythm selections on the portable keyboard.

"I'm usually a piano purist," he confessed with a grin, "but this is fun!"

We began with the suitors' song, "Everyone Goes," which sounded an awful lot like the Cole Porter classic "Anything Goes," but with enough subtle variations to keep things legal and on the up-and-up. Now that I knew about licensing, I had to assume the Drama-o-Rama songwriters had been extremely careful not to mess with copyrights. According to the sheet music, our song was "inspired by" Mr. Porter's.

And of course, the melody made me think of the incredible tap dancing done by the great Patti LuPone, who performed as Reno Sweeney at the 1988 Tony Awards (thank you, YouTube!). I could almost hear the syncopated gunfire sounds of eighteen pairs of tap shoes!

I mentioned this to Maxie; it took her exactly four seconds to come up with the concept of using grosgrain ribbon crisscrossed around the dancers' calves to turn their tap shoes into gladiator sandals! She made a few very impressive sketches.

"How are we doing with the six-headed monster costume?" I asked.

"Working on it," said Maxie, chewing the end of her pencil. "Although I'm thinking it might be more of a casting and blocking concern than a costuming one."

"What do you mean?"

"I've got some ideas, but they're kind of hard to explain." Her eyes sparkled with mystery. "I'll work on some drawings tonight and show you tomorrow."

"Sounds good," I said. We made a plan to sit down with all her artwork—tear sheets, mood boards, and renderings—tomorrow after the bake sale. Deon would join us to discuss his end of the production, although I wasn't sure if he should be focusing on designs for this theater or our own. The safe bet was for him to plan for both, which I knew would be a lot more work for him. But what could we do?

When Austin was satisfied with our rendition of the Porteresque "Everyone Goes" we moved on to "It's All Greek to Me," then "Gotta See a Man About a Horse."

I couldn't believe how awesome the songs were, and how quickly the cast was picking them up.

And before I knew it, rehearsal was over.

"See you all back here tomorrow," I said as the actors gathered up their things. "Start memorizing your lines. We should all be off book by next Monday. And don't forget: have your moms or dads drop off your baked goods at my house sometime during the day tomorrow. We'll all head back there after rehearsal for the sale."

Everyone began to file out of the auditorium. A few of the cast, including my sister, had packed towels and bathing suits and were going to stay and use the indoor pool. I shouted out a reminder for them to shower first, thinking Mrs. Crandall would want it that way.

"Hey, Kenz," I called just before she slipped out the door. "Do you want a ride home? My papa's picking me up, and Susan's seat is open, since she's sticking around to swim."

"That's okay," said Mackenzie. "I've got a ride. I'm meeting my mom at . . . um, in town."

That seemed kind of silly to me. Why would she walk all the way to town to get picked up when she could simply come home in our car and save her mother a trip? But I decided not to question it. Maybe Mrs. Fleisch had errands to run or something.

"Okay," I said. "See you tomorrow."

"Oh, and Anya, I'm sorry but I won't be able to contribute anything to the bake sale. I can help with the selling, but, well, my mom isn't much of a baker, and we don't have cupcake tins or anything."

"That's all right," I said, laughing. "I'm sure between Gracie's baklava and Nora's lemon squares, we'll have plenty."

Mackenzie gave me a weird look, like maybe there was more she wanted to say. But she didn't; she just waved and hurried on her way.

Austin and I went around the entire auditorium to check that the place was as neat and clean as it had been when we'd arrived. I sent Deon and Maxie backstage to do the same. They found some bubble-gum wrappers (Maddie!) and Travis's script. Deon said he'd have his mom swing by Trav's house on their way home and drop it off . . . along with a stern reminder about taking better care of his theatrical materials. When we were satisfied that nothing else had been left behind, we got our stuff, turned off the lights, and headed out of the theater toward the main entrance.

In the lobby, Maxie veered off toward the gym to wait for her little brother to finish basketball camp.

Outside, Deon's mom was already waiting by the curb.

"I'll work on some design elements tonight," D promised, getting into the car. "I'm thinking of bringing in a smoke machine for the Olympus scenes. Ya know, to create a kind of misty, nebulous effect."

"Nebulous," I said, waving to Mrs. Becker. "I like it!"

When Deon was gone, Austin turned to me, a huge smile on his face. "I think we've got a hit on our hands," he declared.

"Me too," I agreed. "The read-through was better than I'd expected, and the songs are incredible. So tomorrow we'll start blocking. Wednesday we can work on fight choreography with Becky and—"

I stopped short when I saw Mackenzie exiting through one of the community center's side doors. She must have made a stop in the ladies' locker room because she'd changed out of her running shorts and T-shirt and into a black leotard and pink tights. Her hair, which had been in a ponytail during rehearsal, was now secured in a flawless ballerina's bun.

As I watched her jog gracefully across the grass and through the parking lot, I realized she wasn't walking toward town at all. She was heading in the complete opposite direction, in fact.

She was heading toward her dance studio.

Just before dinner, Susan knocked on my bedroom door. Her damp hair still smelled of chlorine from her swim at the community center pool, but I barely noticed it because the whole house was filled with fabulous aromas of melting butter, warm vanilla, and brown sugar.

"Smells like Nana's started baking," said Susan, inhaling deeply and making a beeline downstairs to the kitchen. I was hot on her heels.

At the counter, an apron-clad Nana was expertly dropping heaping teaspoons of cookie dough onto a baking sheet. Papa stood beside her, whistling as he reached stealthily for the wooden spoon propped in the mixing bowl.

"Don't you dare lick that spoon, Harold Wallach!" Nana warned, swatting his hand away without looking up from the methodical arrangement of chocolate-studded blobs on the sheet. "There are raw eggs in there! You'll get salmonella or trichinosis or a tapeworm or something."

"Or malaria!" Susan added, helping herself to a handful of tiny candy Kisses. "Or the bubonic plague!"

"Or whooping cough!" Papa joked, sneaking a fully baked cookie off the cooling rack and taking a bite.

"Well, now we know where Susan gets her sense of humor," I said with a grin. "Not to mention her appetite." I took the opened bag of chocolate morsels and moved them deliberately to the far side of the counter, where my sister couldn't reach.

"Now, you girls know Papa and I won't be here for your bake sale, right?"

"We know, Nana," I said. "Tuesday is your hair appointment."

"And how was rehearsal?" asked Nana, sliding the cookie pan into the oven.

"Awesome!" said Susan. "I'm Zeus!"

"Wonderful!" said Nana. "I'll whip you up a nice batch of ambrosia as soon as I'm done with these cookies."

"Thanks for doing all this, Nana," I said, sinking into a kitchen chair. "The bake sale is going to be a big money-maker."

"Speaking of money . . . this arrived for you, Anya," said

Papa, tearing himself away from the cooling rack. He handed me a large manila envelope that jingled a bit. "Sounds like coins. A lad in overalls dropped it off earlier."

"That'd be Matt," I said, pinching the little clasp open and pouring about twelve quarters onto the kitchen table. A bunch of paper money followed, fluttering out like giant confetti.

"I'll count that!" cried Susan as she gleefully joined me at the table and began digging into the pile of bills and change.

I pulled a sheet of paper out of the envelope.

"What have you got there, Anya?" Papa asked. "Looks awfully official."

"It is," I assured him. "It's an ad for our program. This boy, Matt Witten, is promoting his lawn-cutting business."

"He's also a major investor," said Susan.

"I'll say he is!" Papa eyed the bills, clearly surprised at the sum of money. "Seems this young man has a future in big business. You should snap him up, Anya! You two have a lot in common. The two of you could take over the world!"

"Papa!" I said, my face flushing.

"Oh, Anya won't be snapping up Matt Witten," said Susan, carefully separating the twenties from the tens. "She already likes someone else."

Papa smiled. "She does?"

I frowned. "I do?"

Susan looked up from her stacks of cash. "Duh, Anya. You like Austin."

"I do not."

"You do, too."

"I do not! He's my business partner. And my friend."

"Fine." Susan rolled her eyes and started piling the quarters into little pillars of four. "Whatever. Let's see the ad."

Relieved that the topic had shifted, I placed Matt's advertisement in the middle of the table for all of us to admire.

AFFORDABLE AND RELIABLE LAWN CARE
SERVING THE RANDOM FARMS NEIGHBORHOOD
MOWING * WEEDING * GENERAL LANDSCAPING
CALL MATTHEW J. WITTEN
(917) 555-7158
REFERENCES AVAILABLE UPON REQUEST

"Not bad," said Papa. "Short and sweet. Simple and to the point."

"I would have gone with some clip art," said Susan. "A little cartoon lawn mower in the corner would have been cool, or maybe a Weedwacker. Even a rake. Something to spice it up a bit."

"It's fine," I said. "It gets the message across."

As I examined Matt's message, it occurred to me that there was nothing stopping us from taking this ad idea to the next level by creating a whole advertising section in our program!

Numbers began to appear in my head. Prices for full- and half-page ads, rates for black-and-white or color. Selling ad space could bring in a fair amount of profit with a relatively small amount of work. It was just a matter of approaching potential sponsors and convincing them to promote their businesses in our program. How hard could that be? Even with her added responsibilities as Zeus, I was sure Susan could handle the sales component.

But who would we sell ad space *to*? Other than Matt and myself, I didn't know any other kids who were currently operating their own businesses (unless you wanted to count little Hannah Petrova, who sporadically ran a lemonade stand down the street, setting up shop on really hot days, but only if her mother happened to have extra plastic cups in the pantry).

So perhaps I would have to revise my "kids only" thinking to allow for grown-up sponsors. Like Mrs. Taylor, who lived three streets over and marketed herself as an interior design consultant (I knew this because she'd helped Becky's mom redecorate their dining room last winter). Maybe the coffee shop would buy a quarter-page ad. The ice cream parlor, the pizza place . . . They'd been nice enough to let us put posters in their windows; maybe they'd go the extra mile and advertise with us, too.

And then a thought came to me. Mr. Krause, who owned the gas station and mini-mart! As it happened, we shared a mutual business connection. My heart raced because I knew that selling a full-pager to Krause's would accomplish two very significant things:

1) Ka-ching! Ka-ching! And . . .

2) I'd get to talk to Matt again, sooner than later.

This second point made me suddenly realize that Susan's theory about my liking Austin was completely off the mark.

I did like someone.

But it wasn't Austin.

It was Matt.

☆☆☆☆

I used the number from the ad to text Matt. Correction: Matthew J. Witten.

Flopping onto my bed with my iPhone, I began typing.

My first attempt was clunky, to say the least.

Hey, Matt, it's Anya. I need a favor.

My finger hovered over send as I evaluated the message. It seemed a little pushy, maybe even needy. And technically business transactions weren't favors; they were business transactions. But I wasn't conducting business with Matt. I was imposing upon him to approach Mr. Krause on my behalf, so that *was* a favor.

I hit send. A couple of seconds later, my phone dinged.

Hey, Anya. How's it goin'?

I felt a shiver go up my spine. He texted me back! Like, *immediately*. That had to be a good sign. Hands trembling, I repositioned my fingers on the touch screen and typed:

You mentioned you do a lot of business with Mr. Krause.

Ding.

Yep. Why? Is your little sis craving a slushee?

Ding.

LOL.

Okay, now what? Explaining about beefing up the ad section of our program and the fee schedule for different-size advertisements was going to require an awful lot of typing. It would be so much easier just to tell him about it. So I mustered up my courage and typed:

Would you mind if I call you?

I bit my lip, hit send, and then waited for his response.

Ding.

Wouldn't mind at all, LOL. I'd like that.

My eyes went round as I gaped at the glowing screen. He'd like that?

He'd like that!

It wasn't until Susan came bursting through my door in a panic that I realized I'd screamed.

"What's wrong?" she asked, her eyes darting around the room.

"Nothing."

"Jeesh, I thought there was a fire. Or maybe you were trapped under some immovable object or something."

"Well, I'm not. Sorry I scared you. Now get out."

Susan gave me a look but didn't argue. She strode out and shut the door behind her.

Smiling, I took a deep breath.

And I called Matthew J. Witten.

CHAPTER

Our second day of rehearsal went smoothly; we marched through the play, scene by scene, to establish a general sense of blocking and pacing, noting where the songs and dance numbers would come in. I loved the news anchor shtick where the Greek chorus filled in the audience on all the events leading up to the Trojan War. Throughout the play, their job would be to report on Odysseus's situation in the form of "breaking-news updates."

There was one moment in which Kenzie interviewed the six-headed beast Scylla, as played by Spencer, which was hilarious because a second monster, Charybdis (Jane), who was basically defined as a swirling pool of water, kept trying to interrupt.

It was instantly clear that the costuming for these characters would have to be highly original, even beyond the creative ingenuity of repurposed bath mats.

So I went backstage to where Maxie was working on wardrobe sketches, and asked her what she was thinking with regard to Scylla.

"I was stumped at first," she confessed. "I was thinking maybe there was a way I could attach five masks to Spencer's shoulders, but I realized that would be way too uncomfortable. So I came up with a plan to have Spencer stand in the middle of the stage and put five other actors around him, three on individual risers, and two kneeling, so their heads would be arranged at varying heights."

"I like it," I said, picturing the image.

"They'll be dressed all in black, and I'll have Deon darken the stage, lighting only their faces. Well, and, of course, Spencer's whole body. This way they'll appear to be these creepy disembodied heads just hovering around him. I'm thinking they'll have tangled wigs and horrible fangs."

"That's visionary!" I cried. "D, can we achieve that effect?"

"We can *here*," he said, pointing to the lights. "But I'm afraid it won't translate to the clubhouse. We don't have that many spotlights."

I frowned, but Maxie barreled on, undeterred.

"I sort of figured that would be the case," she said. "So if we are back in the clubhouse for the show, I'll give each extra head a flashlight to shine under his or her chin."

"Uplighting," said Deon. "Spooky. And easy. Very clever."

"Thanks." Maxie beamed with pride. "I was hoping you'd like it."

"I really do," I said. "But what about Charybdis, the whirlpool?"

"That's kind of a surprise," said Maxie. "Jane and I are having a meeting at my house tonight after the bake sale to work on it."

"Perfect," I said. "Can you give me a hint?"

"It involves an old toy I had to con my little brother out of," she said with a mysterious grin. "But that's all I'm saying for now."

Since I didn't want to mess with her creative brilliance, I decided not to push it. I trusted her completely, and besides, it was time to head back to my house.

We had a bake sale to run!

✧✦✩✦✩

"Cookies! Cupcakes! Brownies!" cried Susan in her best leader-of-the-gods voice. "Get 'em while they last."

"At this rate," Deon muttered, "they might last forever."

Sadly, D was right. Sales were discouragingly slow to the

point of being nearly nonexistent, though it wasn't for a lack of preparedness.

Susan had tweeted about the fund-raiser, Brittany had used poster board to make two large hand-lettered **BAKE SALE** signs, and we'd set up two card tables at the end of the driveway that we covered with brightly colored cloths. Our wide array of yummy, frosted wares was artfully arranged on paper plates and plastic platters, and if I do say so myself, we had a very impressive supply.

Unfortunately, I'd seriously overestimated the demand.

It occurred to me that perhaps the large amount of people we'd seen on the street last Sunday was more of a weekend phenomenon. Today was Tuesday, and there was far less activity. I realized now that our neighbors were probably anxious to get home after a long day at work; even the kids were probably tired after seven hours at sports camp or parks and rec programs. The few cars and bikes that did go by didn't even slow down.

"I don't get it," said Austin. "Why isn't anyone buying?"

"What a waste of time," said Susan, eyeing the lemon bars with interest. "If we'd known this was going to be such a bust, we could have stayed at the community center and kept rehearsing."

"I suppose we could cut our losses and go over a few

more songs," I said glumly.

And then something my grandfather had mentioned came crashing back into my head.

"That's it!" I cried. "It's so Broadway!"

"What is?" asked Susan. "What are you talking about?"

"You know all Papa's stories about how in the old days, when Broadway producers wanted to test a new show, they would have a preview at the Shubert Theater in New Haven?"

"Yeah." Susan gave me a skeptical look. "Are you saying you want us to try selling these cookies up in Connecticut?"

"No," said Austin, getting it now. "She wants us to have a preview. She wants us to put on part of the show . . . but not at the Shubert . . . right here in the front yard."

"Eighteen kids singing and dancing are bound to get people's attention!" I said. "They'll stop to watch!"

"Or they'll stop to tell us to quit disturbing the peace," said Susan.

"I don't think so," I said. "I think they'll be curious and excited. And as long as they're here, I'm betting they'll buy something to snack on."

"I agree," said Austin. "Besides, what can it hurt? Worst-case scenario, we get in a little extra practice. I say we give it a shot."

We quickly gathered everyone around the bake sale table

and explained our strategy. Then Austin counted them in, and they broke into a wonderful a cappella version of "It's All Greek to Me."

Our timing couldn't have been better. Mr. Davenport, who was once again walking by with Patches, stopped to listen to us. To our surprise, Patches threw back his furry head and howled right along with the music. The truly funny thing was that, as far as I could tell, Patches was howling on key.

"Too bad he doesn't know the words," quipped Austin.

"We'll have to keep him in mind if we ever *do* put on *Annie*," I observed, sweeping my hand in an arc gesture to indicate a marquee. "Starring Patches Davenport as 'Sandy.' "

"Excellent casting choice," said Susan. "I'll get his agent on the phone right now."

When the song ended, in appreciation of our efforts, Mr. Davenport bought a red velvet cupcake. Even better than that—he fished his cell phone out of the pocket of his plaid Bermuda shorts and called his wife.

"C'mon over to the Wallachs' place," he told her. "The kids are doing some kind of theatrical preview. They're darn good, too. And bring your purse. . . . There's a peach cobbler I've got my eye on."

"It's working!" said Susan.

"Brady, sing Poseidon's song," I directed. "And project!"

Brady did exactly that. Sure enough, doors and windows up and down the street began to open. A group of kids on skateboards came coasting around the corner. When they saw the baked goods, their eyes lit up. As Brady did his best surfer-dude rendition of the sea god's solo, they, too, pulled out their cell phones to spread the word.

Mrs. Davenport, who'd been hosting her bridge club when she'd gotten her husband's call, showed up during the second verse, along with three other ladies from the neighborhood. They all seemed delighted to be getting an impromptu performance on a Tuesday afternoon, and happily plunked down payment for the cherry cheesecake Maddie's mother had contributed.

I hastily posted Gina by the mailbox to remind people to save the date for our next performance.

"Should I tell them we're having it at the community center?" she asked.

"No. There's still a good chance the clubhouse will be ready, and I think we should remain optimistic."

"Cautiously optimistic," Austin clarified. "Now, let's sing."

"Gotta See a Man About a Horse" was next in the lineup, and soon the street was filled with people enjoying our preview and purchasing goodies.

And then, from the direction of the clubhouse, a

battalion of city workers appeared in their yellow hard hats, reflective orange safety vests, and muddy work boots. As they came strutting down Random Farms Circle in the fading summer light, they looked like a proud and powerful army on the march. If we were in a movie, I was pretty sure such a dramatic entrance would have been filmed in slow motion.

"Uh-oh," said Susan. "I bet our performance was bothering them while they were trying to work."

"They use jackhammers and steamrollers," I reminded her. "We're singing show tunes. How could *we* bother *them*?" But I felt a little tremor of panic. Maybe we *were* in for a scolding.

The foreman of the crew approached the card table. His muscular forearms were streaked with tar. "I hear there's a bunch of kids who're anxious to be back in that clubhouse we're working on. Are you that gang?"

"You must be thinking of *West Side Story*," said Susan nervously. "We aren't a gang; we're a theater troupe."

Austin shut her up with an elbow to the ribs.

"Yes, sir," I confirmed. "We're those kids."

The foreman took off his hard hat and grinned. "Well, I just want you to know we're going to do our best to make that happen. No promises, but we're giving it our all."

"We also heard you're selling cookies," said a burly man

with a gray mustache. "How much for one of those snicker-doodles?"

I was about to tell him the price when Susan stepped in front of me and quickly handed Mustache Guy a handful of cookies. "For you, gentlemen, they're on the house," she said, smiling brightly.

"No, no," said the foreman. "This is a fund-raiser. We want to do our part. I've got a daughter studying theater at the Tisch School in Manhattan. So I get what it means to be a struggling artist."

"We appreciate that," I said, smiling. "Try the baklava. It's outstanding."

As Susan doled out the treats and Austin counted change, I ran inside to grab the CD player and the sound track Drama-o-Rama had provided, to add a little more flash to our performance.

As the neighbors and workmen munched on coconut bars, blondies, and iced sugar cookies, they were given a preview I was sure even the Shubert brothers would have been proud of. Sophia sang her Cyclops solo, then Maddie, Jane, and Elle got their Motown on by totally nailing the Sirens' song. The crowd applauded wildly.

And thanks to the hearty appetites of the work crew, we had nearly sold out of goodies.

"Shall we give them a grand finale?" I whispered to Austin.

His reply was to hit the play button. The instrumental track of "Everyone Goes" filled the air.

The cast arranged themselves in a long line, their arms interlocked behind one another's backs.

"Right foot first!" Mackenzie called out. "Five, six, seven, eight . . ."

Our customers watched in awe as my dancers executed a flawless kickline. Even I was impressed, since they'd really only had one chance to rehearse it. Then Kenzie called out to some of the little kids who were watching and invited them to link themselves to the ends of the line.

Their moms cheered as these tiny new recruits fell into step (well, sort of) with the rest of the dancers.

"Future Random Farms cast members," Austin said, laughing.

"Future dues payers," Susan said, rubbing her palms together and beaming.

When the song finished, everyone was laughing breathlessly.

As the workmen went back to the clubhouse, Mackenzie and I sold the few remaining goodies to the audience at a discount; they all expressed their hope that the theater would be ready in time for our second show.

Everyone was in a terrific mood . . . until a silver sedan pulled up to the curb.

I recognized the car immediately. It belonged to Mrs. Fleisch.

Mackenzie, who was handing our last brownie to a customer, dropped it like it was on fire. Her face went completely pale. When Mrs. Fleisch got out of the car, I could see her expression was one of pure fury.

I had no idea what Mackenzie's mother was so upset about, but as she stomped across the grass, one thing was perfectly clear. . . .

She wasn't here to buy a cookie.

"Mackenzie Allison Fleisch, what in the world are you doing?"

Mackenzie opened her mouth to answer, but no sound came out. Didn't matter; Mrs. Fleisch was clearly in talking, not listening, mode.

"I called the dance studio to let them know I'd be picking you up early today. I almost had a heart attack when Miss Juliette told me you weren't there."

I wondered if Mrs. Fleisch's potential coronary had to do with the fact that Mackenzie was missing . . . or just that she was missing dance class.

"I can . . . um . . . Let me just . . . I can explain," Mackenzie stammered.

But Mrs. Fleisch continued as though she wasn't aware half the neighborhood was watching. "I told Juliette she simply had to be mistaken, because you had an advanced pas de deux class scheduled for four thirty. But she told me you hadn't shown up for it. And then she went on to tell me that you weren't there yesterday, either. In fact, your attendance has been spotty all summer!" Mrs. Fleisch gave her daughter a disappointed look. "Spotty, Mackenzie! Do you think when Anna Pavlova was twelve years old, *her* attendance was ever *spotty*?"

"Anna Pavlova," Susan whispered to me. "Lemonade stand, right?"

"No," I whispered back. "Shhh!"

"I did go to the studio this morning," Mackenzie said, "just like I told you I was going to do. I rehearsed all day. But not in class. I worked independently. I guess Miss Juliette didn't realize I was there."

"Why would you do that?"

Mackenzie swallowed hard and I realized she was stalling. Correction: *lying!*

"Because," Mackenzie said at last, not quite meeting her mother's gaze. "Because Desiree Morton is in all those same classes, and you know how awful she is to me. She always tries to psyche me out and make me feel self-conscious."

"Yes." Mrs. Fleisch pursed her lips and nodded. "She does do that."

"I thought if I could just practice on my own," Mackenzie went on, "I'd be able to focus on my dancing without Desiree playing head games and messing me up. So I found an empty practice room and spent the day working there."

Not true, I thought, feeling queasy. *She spent the day with us at the CCC.*

"But what about pas de deux?" Mrs. Fleisch countered. "You certainly can't practice *that* by yourself!"

This time Mackenzie didn't miss a beat. "Vladimir texted me and told me he was skipping class," she said easily. "I didn't tell Juliette because I didn't want him to get in trouble. But since I wasn't going to have a class partner, I didn't see any point in staying. So I got a ride home from Annabelle's mom, but because there's so much construction at the east end of Random Farms Circle, I just had her drop me off at the corner and I walked. Jogged actually. To burn more calories."

At this, Mrs. Fleisch actually looked pleased.

"That was when I saw Anya was having a bake sale, so I stopped to help out. I've been here only a few minutes."

I kept my eyes fixed firmly on the card table because I didn't dare look at Mrs. Fleisch, or for that matter, Mackenzie. I was sure my shock was as plain as the nose on my face. This had to be one of the most exquisitely detailed lies ever told.

"Please don't tell on Vlad," Kenzie went on, her voice

catching dramatically. "He's such a good partner and he's the best male dancer at the studio. I don't want to get him mad. He might start dancing with Desiree instead of me."

At this statement, I couldn't help but sneak a glance at Kenzie's mom. She looked horrified at the thought of this Desiree person stealing away her daughter's pas de deux partner. Finally she shook her head, as though dismissing the entire incident.

"Get in the car, Mackenzie," Mrs. Fleisch instructed. "I've managed to get you into a special class tonight in Manhattan. We're going straight to the train."

Without another word, Mackenzie gathered up her things and bolted for the car.

But as Mrs. Fleisch strode around to the driver's door, I heard this:

"I hope you haven't eaten any of those baked goods. Have you seen the dancers in New York? They're positively svelte."

"What's *svelte*?" Susan whispered.

I didn't know. But for some reason, it sounded like one of the ugliest words I'd ever heard in my life.

☆☆☆

No one said a word.

Even though it was clear Mackenzie had just blatantly lied to her mother about where she'd been for the last two days (not to mention the entire first session of the Random Farms Kids' Theater), nobody, it seemed, had the stomach to say it out loud.

I certainly didn't. The two lemon bars I'd eaten earlier were suddenly churning in my belly, creating a whirlpool worthy of Charybdis. I felt positively sick. And not just because Mackenzie had proven herself to be the most amazing liar in the entire world.

But because I was a very close second.

☆⭐☆⭐

"Hi, Mom."

"Anya! *Ma chérie!*"

"How's Paris?"

"It's wonderful! Dad and I are getting ready to go out for an elegant dinner."

"That's great." I paused, picturing a swath of awkward silence forming across the Atlantic Ocean. Even with several time zones between us, my mother knew something was up.

"Anya, what's wrong? Did something happen?"

The fear in her voice made me feel even worse than I already did.

"Everything's fine," I said quickly. "Nobody's hurt or anything. There's just something I wanted to tell you. Can you put me on speaker so Dad can hear?"

The phone fumbled a bit, then I heard my father's equally worried voice. "I'm here, Anya. What's going on?"

I took a deep breath. "I was dishonest with you guys, and I lied to Nana and Papa." My throat felt tight and there was a stinging sensation behind my eyes. "I'm sorry. I know it was wrong. But I really needed a place to hold rehearsals while the clubhouse was closed down, and when the Paris trip came up, I knew if I could convince Mom to go, I'd be able to have rehearsals at home and you'd never know. When the kids came for auditions, I kind of led Nana and Papa to believe that I had your permission."

More grim silence filled the atmosphere between the two continents. Finally I heard my father sigh.

"This isn't like you, Anya. You've never lied to us before."

"I know," I said. "But I was desperate. I told myself I really wouldn't be breaking the rules, because we wouldn't be bothering Mom while she was working. And even though it was supposed to be two weeks, it was only those first two days. After the flood we—"

"Flood?" cried my mother.

"It's fine now," I assured her. "We cleaned it up and the washer is working again."

My mother gasped and I heard my father whisper something to her before turning the conversation back to me. "And what about your play? I assume you were forced to call it off?"

"Not exactly," I said. Then I explained all about the community center and Matt Witten's ad and the bake sale.

He was quiet again, and I realized I was waiting for him to tell me I shouldn't have bothered going to all that trouble because he fully intended to exercise his parental rights and teach me a lesson by canceling not only this play, but any show I dreamed of ever producing in the future.

To be honest, if I were *my* kid, that was what *I* would have done.

When at last my father spoke, I heard a tone of uncertainty in his voice. "On the one hand, I'm impressed by your ability to troubleshoot. You had a problem, and you found an intelligent solution by renting the community center theater. That is a skill you can be proud of."

"Thank you."

"But on the other hand, you were dishonest, not only with me and your mother, but with your grandparents as well."

My head bowed of its own accord as tears welled up in my eyes.

"And even though the washing machine debacle was taken care of, things could have gone very differently."

"I know," I said, my voice little more than a croak. "So I guess I'm going to be punished, right?"

"*Absolument*," said Mom.

I didn't speak French but I knew a *darn right!* when I heard one. My heart went cold. "Do I have to cancel the show?"

More whispers. I held my breath.

"This is going to involve further discussion on our part," said Dad. "Your mother and I will have to think long and hard about this, Anya. We'll let you know our decision when we get home."

For one frantic moment I considered begging, reminding them how much I loved my theater and explaining that the thought of not having a second play had resulted in a touch of temporary insanity.

But instead I simply said, "Okay." The word was lost in a sob.

I hit end on my cell phone, feeling dizzy.

Friday! Three whole days before I'd learn my fate.

Once again I felt like Odysseus. He was always at the

mercy of the gods who held his hopes, his dreams, his very life in their hands. His future was determined by their whims, just as mine would be determined by my parents' decision.

Of course, Odysseus was a brave and noble hero.

And I was just a big selfish liar!

Would there be a second show or wouldn't there? And what was I supposed to do for the next three days? Cancel rehearsals or carry on, as Odysseus did? He had a responsibility to his men, just like I was responsible to my actors. And I didn't want to let them down any more than Odysseus had wanted to see his buddies get gobbled by Scylla or pounded against the rocks by Poseidon.

I could keep it to myself until I knew for sure, but wouldn't that be lying all over again?

Feeling miserable, I curled up on my bed, my Broadway playlist blasting through my earbuds, and started counting the minutes until Friday.

The next morning, Papa drove us to the community center. I felt anxious and confused, wondering how much of my current problem I should reveal to the cast. As we picked up the rest of our car pool riders, I kept telling myself that my parents were kind, rational people. Even if they did decide I should be punished, they'd never be heartless enough to punish my entire cast along with me. I'd simply point out to Mom and Dad how hard everyone had been working and how unfair it would be to take the play away from *them* when *I* was the one who'd made the bad judgment call.

This line of reasoning bolstered my spirits a bit. By the time we pulled up to the CCC entrance, I was actually smiling. Because it was Wednesday and that meant Becky would be joining us to help choreograph the battle scenes.

Even though I'd felt a little strange about it at first, I was

Stagestruck: Showstopper!

really excited now. My best friend and I had never taken part in an activity together. This was long overdue.

She was waiting in the lobby, a huge grin on her face and an envelope in her hand.

"What's that?" I asked.

"Special delivery. Open it."

I slid open the flap and pulled out a piece of letter-size paper; folded inside it was a check made out to Random Farms Kids' Theater for the cost of a full-page ad. My heart sped up as I read the advertisement.

> FOR THE BEST PRICES AND MOST RELIABLE SERVICE
> CHOOSE KRAUSE'S FILLING STATION
> AND MINI-MART
> BEST PRICES IN TOWN ON GAS AND GROCERIES
> *"FILL YOUR TANK OR STOCK YOUR HOUSE—*
> *FOR ONE-STOP SHOPPING, COME TO KRAUSE."*

I couldn't believe it. Matt had told me on the phone he was pretty sure Mr. Krause would contribute an ad. I never imagined he'd handle it so quickly.

But here it was! I felt a surge of hope. How could my parents cancel a show that was being sponsored by the guy

160

who sold the lowest-priced gasoline in town?

I folded the ad and slipped both it and the check back into the envelope, which I tucked carefully into my tote bag.

"How'd you get it?" I asked Becky.

"Matt swung by to drop it off a few minutes ago," she said with a wag of her eyebrows. "And he seemed very disappointed at not being able to hand it to you in person."

I felt a huge smile spreading across my face.

"Okay, everyone," I said, herding my cast from the lobby to the theater. "Let's get moving. This show goes up in two and a half weeks."

I hope.

✩✩✩✩✩

Because Becky had never been the sort to leave things to chance, she'd spent all her downtime over the last few days Googling "stage combat." She'd also consulted with two of her older brothers, Ben—a high-school track star whose best event was the javelin—and Charlie, who took fencing as an elective in college. Not only had Charlie given his sister a crash course in swordplay, he'd also allowed her to borrow some equipment to use for today's rehearsal.

"What are those?" asked Travis, indicating the two long,

slim weapons Becky was holding.

"This one's a foil," Becky explained. "And this is an épée. They aren't sharp or pointy, and they're really flexible." She demonstrated the bendy quality of the foil by pressing its tip to my solar plexus. "See how it arcs? And the end is blunted, which is why Anya isn't bleeding to death right now."

"Cool," said Travis.

"Two skinny swords isn't much of an arsenal," Austin observed. "Maxie?"

"Not a problem," said Maxie. "The play kit was really helpful about props. They listed all sorts of websites that sell stage weapons, and there's a promo code for Drama-o-Rama customers that will get us a pretty good discount."

"Good," I said. Even with the Krause filling station full-pager, we were still operating on a budget. "Let's meet after rehearsal to discuss that," I suggested, eager to get to the actual stage combat. I was looking forward to seeing my bestie in action. "We'll start with these two. Everyone else can just mime for now."

The cast assembled onstage, including the stage crew, since they'd be playing suitors and warriors. The play called for a major battle scene to take place between Odysseus and the suitors upon his return to Ithaca. My vision was that the battle would be executed as part knock-down, drag-out brawl, part dance number. Mackenzie would be a featured performer in both, taking on most of the dance parts; she and Becky were going to work together to find just the right balance between grace and grit.

Odysseus and Telemachus (Teddy and Spencer, respectively) stood downstage right, while their enemies, Antinous and Eurymachus (Brady and Jane), positioned themselves downstage left, just as we'd blocked it the day before.

"The gist of this scene is that Odysseus has come home at last," I reminded them. "He's disguised as a beggar, thanks to Athena, and only his son, Telemachus, knows who he is." I nodded to Austin to continue the summary.

"You've all read the script, so you know that Penelope has had it up to here with the suitors, and since at this point she's pretty sure her husband is history, she's resigned herself to choosing one of the obnoxious guys to take his place."

"That's not very romantic," said Sophia.

"No," I conceded, "but it does make for a really thrilling action scene. And speaking of action scenes . . ."

On this cue Becky got down to business.

For most of the rehearsal things went smoothly, since we had only two weapons to contend with. But at one point Elle zigged when she should have zagged, just as Nora bobbed when she should have weaved, which sent Teddy shuffling left when he should have been skittering right; unfortunately, this all resulted in Sophia accidentally taking a foil to the back of the head.

"Hey, watch the hair!" she shouted.

"Sorry," Teddy muttered.

But as the battle raged on, it became clear that blunted or not, a poorly aimed stage weapon could definitely do some damage. I tried to imagine the ruckus of ducking and spinning and parrying and thrusting when we had not just two but more than a dozen actors wielding actual (fake) spears, clubs, and swords. It had the potential to be like the worst piñata experience ever! I could practically hear my mother shrieking in terror, *It's all fun and games until someone gets hurt*, and, of course, that old parental favorite, *Somebody is going to lose an eye!*

Austin came to the same conclusion. "We're going to have to be dead-on with this fight choreography," he whispered. "Or else take out an insurance policy."

"I agree," I said.

When Becky told her warriors to "take five," I waved her over and whispered my concerns.

"Don't worry," she said. "I was thinking the same thing, since I'd feel horrible if anyone got hurt doing something I taught them."

I knew this was true because when we were six, she'd tried to teach me to do a cartwheel, and I wound up spraining my wrist; she'd cried harder than I had!

"So what do the YouTube tutorials and Drama-o-Rama people recommend for directors who don't happen to have Zorro on speed dial?" I asked.

Becky laughed. "They strongly suggest fight calls."

"Fight calls?" I repeated. "You mean, like, 'Charge!'?"

Becky shook her head. "In professional theater, actors performing stage combat are obligated to have what's known as a fight call before every single performance. It's basically a mandatory extra rehearsal of the fight choreography for the purpose of knowing it cold and leaving nothing to chance."

That made sense. After all, a single mistimed step, stumble, or stab (even with phony weaponry) could be a really big deal. Knowing the choreography by heart and having the timing memorized down to the split second would go a long way toward keeping the actors from getting hurt, either by inadvertently tripping over one another or accidentally taking a swat to the gut.

"We'll definitely allow for fight calls in the rehearsal schedule," I said.

Knowing the actors would be so well prepared was a huge relief. I tore a page from my notepad and wrote down a number. "Here's what we can afford to spend on weapons," I said, handing this dollar amount to Maxie. "Anything that costs more than that we'll have to do without. And make sure you get the shipping details. We're going to need these by next week if we want to rehearse with them before the show."

"Gotcha," said Maxie.

When the cast returned from their break, Becky and Mackenzie spent the rest of the day matching the performers' actions to the raucous series of loud metallic clanking on the sound effects CD, which Deon played from the theater's state-of-the-art sound booth.

The auditorium was alive with whooshing, scraping, ringing, and crashing noises. It really did sound as if the actors were in the heat of battle. In a few spots, there were even sounds of spears whizzing through the air or swords being pulled out of sheaths, so Becky and Mackenzie needed to be sure they allowed for corresponding movements at just the right moments.

"It's really not all that different from getting a dance step to happen on a particular beat," Mackenzie observed. "Just imagine the swords and spears 'dancing' to the 'music' of the sound effects."

It was good advice and it worked. After a few more tries, the "warriors" were able to mime their actions in perfect sync with the sounds.

"How are we going to make this happen in the clubhouse," Austin asked me, keeping his voice low, "if we don't have a PA system?"

"We might not even have a clubhouse," Susan replied grimly.

Or a director, I added silently. *If my parents decide to ground me for the rest of my life.*

CHAPTER 16

By the end of rehearsal on Thursday we'd managed to make it through the entire first act of the play without any major snags. But not without a little drama.

I noticed that Travis, who'd been such an enthusiastic Athena at auditions, seemed to have lost a bit of his zeal. He hit his marks and said his lines, but there was a stiffness and a self-consciousness to his performance that hadn't been there before.

After his first scene with Odysseus, I pulled him aside.

"What's up, Trav?" I asked gently. "You seem a little . . . I dunno . . . reluctant to put your heart into it or something."

Travis shrugged, unwilling to meet my eyes.

"Are you not feeling the same energy from Teddy that you had with Mackenzie when she was your scene partner?" I prompted.

"Nah. That's not it. Teddy's a great Odysseus. It's just . . ."

I waited. Travis let out a long rush of breath.

"Well, I was telling some of my friends I'd be playing a goddess in the show, and they started goofin' on me pretty bad. Ya know . . . for dressing up like a girl. I told them all that stuff Austin taught us about guys playing ladies' roles in Shakespearean times, but they just laughed harder."

"Oh." I forced myself to appear calm, but inside, I was on the verge of panic. Why did boys have to be such . . . such . . . *cavemen*? Still, I understood Travis's hesitation. Nobody wanted to get hassled by his friends for any reason.

"So . . . are you going to quit?" I asked.

Again Travis shrugged. My stomach flipped over.

This was *not* good. I hated the idea of losing Travis as Athena, not only because he was awesome, but because recasting his part would mean completely adjusting the complicated web of dual casting choices we'd worked out. More important, I wanted to see him stand up to his friends and do what he knew was right, which was to play the role he'd been given.

Then again I didn't want Travis to feel uncomfortable, and (perhaps a bit selfishly) I didn't want a lackluster portrayal of Athena to undermine our show. So it was on the tip of my tongue to suggest he switch roles with Susan, and play Zeus instead, when my sister's voice exploded behind me.

"Tom Hanks, Tyler Perry, Adam Sandler, Dustin Hoffman."

Travis and I whirled to see my sister holding out her iPhone.

"Just Googled it," she said in her booming Zeus voice. "A list of big-time actors who've played women's roles in movies and gotten huge accolades for doing it. Think any of your buddies would ever have the guts to laugh in *their* faces?"

"No," Travis conceded.

"Didn't think so," said Susan. "So who cares what they think? Trust me, Trav, you're going to be hilarious as Athena."

"I agree with Zeus . . . uh, I mean Susan," I said.

Travis looked deeply pleased by our show of faith.

"Okay," he said at last. "I'll do it. I'm having fun, so why should I let those jerks ruin it for me?"

When he was gone, Susan gave me a cocky smile. "And *that's* how we do it on Mount Olympus," she said.

☆°☆°✩

On Friday we kicked things off with our first official "fight call." This consisted of reviewing the stage combat basics we'd learned the day before, then practicing the choreography Mackenzie and Becky had created. Mackenzie was going to have a featured role in the battle scene, performing a highly imaginative hybrid of jazz dancing and stage combat.

The actors mimed their actions in perfect sync with the sound effects of clanking swords and whooshing spears. They were becoming so proficient, I could almost see their weapons slicing through the air. When Odysseus and Antinous struggled with swords locked in battle, I could have sworn I was seeing the motion of the steel. The invisible weapons gave the fight scene a ghostly, magical quality.

Then Sophia blew us away with her Cyclops solo. The girl was really getting in touch with her inner monster! She stomped around the stage and growled out her song so believably, I was beginning to fear she'd have trouble getting into the more ethereal and feminine Circe character.

But she nailed that, too. Joey (who was really getting the hang of the lyre) accompanied her as she belted out the sultry witch's song, which was a sassy little number called "Men Are Pigs!" It was a riot!

"I hate to say this," I whispered to Austin, "but I'm starting to develop some serious professional respect for Sophia."

"I was just thinking the same thing," said Austin. "You can't ignore that kind of talent."

Unfortunately, my "professional respect" took a serious hit when I heard Sophia attempting to bait Nora into an argument over whether Odysseus should have stayed with Circe or gone home to Penelope.

"Circe is a goddess," Sophia huffed. "Penelope is a housewife. It's a no-brainer."

"Penelope's royalty," Nora pointed out calmly.

"Circe is gorgeous!"

"So is Penelope. She's also faithful and resourceful and doesn't turn people into farm animals."

Sophia's eyes flashed, and she leaned in so her nose was almost touching Nora's. "Fine," she said. "But just remember this. Circe is immortal, which means she was around long before Penelope, and she'll be around long after." Then she planted her hands on her hips and added, "Plus, Circe is a way better singer!"

As Sophia stomped off, I realized the heated debate I'd just witnessed had nothing to do with Circe or Penelope at all. This was about Sophia reminding Nora that she'd been a Random Farms member first and she was not about to take a backseat to a new girl.

Rivalry. I supposed it was unavoidable. I told myself Sophia would get over it before the show and turned my attention back to rehearsal.

Brady's turn. He was outstanding when he delivered his Poseidon monologue.

Somehow he'd found the perfect balance between angry god and swaggering beach bum, and managed to make it believable.

As Austin and I watched Brady's scene from the third row, Deon came and slipped into a seat behind us.

"I've got a really cool idea," he said.

"Let's hear it," said Austin.

"I want to light Poseidon—I mean Brady—entirely in blue and green. Whenever he's on the stage, it'll be lit with aquamarine sea tones."

"Go for it!" I told D, then called out to Brady onstage, "Hold up a second."

"Something wrong?"

"Not at all. Just give Deon a minute to get to the lighting board."

Brady shrugged and lazily twirled his freshly painted trident. A moment later the entire stage was bathed in a pale bluish-green glow.

"It looks like he's underwater!" cried Elle.

"That's awesome," said Joey. "Hey, wasn't there a 'Waves' track on the sound effects CD?" He put down the lyre and joined D in the booth to fiddle with the sound board. Suddenly the theater was filled with the sounds of a crashing surf.

"I love it!" I said. "Okay, Brady. Again. From the top."

As Poseidon launched into his monologue, Susan came and plopped down onto the seat beside me. She had a strange look on her face, as though she were disgusted with something. Or someone.

"The show's really coming along great," I said. "Isn't it?"

"Yep."

"Look at that lighting! Makes it kind of hard to believe we aren't actually adrift in the middle of the Aegean, huh?"

"Yep."

I turned to frown at her. "What's the matter?"

"You're turning into a lotus-eater. That's what's the matter!"

"I'm *what*?"

"Act two, scene four!" she snapped. "Odysseus tells the Greek chorus all about this island where his men were fed these weird, magical lotus flowers that made them all dreamy and kind of stupid."

I gasped. "Are you calling me stupid?"

In response, she opened her script and showed me the scene. "Read it and weep, sister!"

Odysseus: The lotus flowers were so delicious, the men stopped caring about getting home. They were delirious and content. All they wanted was to stay and gobble up the blossoms forever, without even thinking about their return.

I handed back the script and raised an eyebrow at her. "So?"

"Don't you get it?" Susan shook her head in exasperation. "Anya, this theater is the island, and the lights and the sound system are the lotus flowers. *You're* the lotus-eater! All you can see is how great the stage and the curtains and the equipment are, and you're forgetting all about home. *Our* home! The clubhouse! With the Christmas lights stapled to the stage and the curtain made of Mrs. Quandt's old bed linens and no microphones. Remember, Anya?"

This time I *did* feel as though I'd been hit with a Zeusian lightning bolt. In one blinding flash my sister had brought me back to reality.

I *was* a lotus-eater! I'd grown so distracted by this fully functioning theater that I'd allowed myself to put everything else out of my mind. Sure, the lights were cool, and the sound was amazing, but as Susan had just pointed out—as Odysseus surely would have known from the start—the community center wasn't home. It was a port in a storm, a pleasant diversion, an island on the way from Troy to Ithaca.

But it wasn't where we truly belonged.

The clubhouse theater was ours. We'd found it, fixed it up, and made it an awesome place. But even more important than all of that was that at the clubhouse, we called the shots.

We didn't have to answer to anyone. The grown-ups at the CCC had been helpful and pleasant, but the whole point of Random Farms was to create a theater run entirely by kids. That wasn't the case here. Here we were at the mercy of someone else's schedule and rules.

How could I have forgotten that?

"Okay, people," I said loudly, "change of plans. Deon, the lights look incredible and the sound is fantastic. But we have to figure out if any of it can be re-created at the clubhouse. Because that's where we want to be! That's what we're still hoping for. So anything that can't be done back at Random Farms will have to be out."

Brady looked confused. "So no more blue lights?"

"Only if Deon can figure out a way to achieve the same effect in *our* theater. He's a technical genius, so I'm sure he'll come up with some alternative—if not something exactly the same, at least something close."

"You're willing to settle for close?" asked Gracie. "That's what you want?"

"No," I said simply. "What I want is to go back to the clubhouse theater where we can do what we want to do, how and when we want to do it. What I want is to go home."

"That's an excellent idea," said a familiar voice from the back of the theater.

Chapter Sixteen

I turned to see Mom and Dad in the doorway, home from Paris and ready to discuss my punishment.

"Anya," said Mom, crooking her finger, "it's time for you to come home."

Talk about getting back to reality.

All things considered, I would have preferred the lightning bolt.

✩✩✩✩✩

I left Austin in charge and made my way slowly up the center aisle.

Susan had already run ahead to welcome our parents back with a big hug. Then she met me halfway and whispered, "What's going on?"

"I told them everything," I whispered back. "The basement rehearsal, the washing machine . . . all of it. They've had three days to decide what to do with me. That's why I'm going home. To find out what my punishment's going to be."

Susan's face went pale. "Do you think they'd—"

"They might." I gave her a stern look. "But don't tell anyone. Not yet. I don't want to worry them if I don't have to. It might still be okay. And they've all worked so hard."

Susan surprised me with a grin. "You really are like

Odysseus," she said. "You want to protect your men. Well, boys. And girls. But you get the point. It's heroic."

That made me feel a little better. But only a little.

"Make sure Austin helps Spencer with his speech to the suitors," I reminded her. "He needs to sound angrier. And Nora needs to come off a little sneakier in her scene with Antinous. Have her work on that."

"Will do. And, Anya . . . good luck."

I gave my sister the best smile I could muster and continued up the aisle, feeling a little envious of old Odysseus. All he had to do was outsmart the gods and navigate the dangerous straits between the vicious and formidable pair of sea monsters, Scylla and Charybdis.

What I had to deal with was more frightening and unpredictable: a pair of disappointed parents.

And you didn't have to be a student of Greek tragedy to know there was nothing more nerve-wracking than that!

☆✲☆☆

We rode home in silence.

I probably should have asked them how their trip was, but I couldn't get the words out. I was a nervous wreck. I feared that if I opened my mouth, the only thing I'd be able to say would be, *Are you going to let me do the play?*

So I sat in the backseat with my hands folded and didn't say a word.

Just as we turned into the driveway, my phone gave a little chirp. It was a text message from Ms. Napolitano, the special events coordinator at the CCC, confirming that I had paid in full to reserve the theater for the following week. She also asked if I still wanted to keep it on hold for the week after that.

I texted back:

Yes, please, keep the theater on hold.

She wrote back that she would do so, but reminded me that payment would be due before the end of business next Friday, in order for us to be allowed into the theater on Monday morning.

I was about to put a reminder alert in my iCalendar when Dad cut the engine.

Tucking the phone into my tote bag, I got out of the car and followed my parents inside.

✩✿ ✩✩

We went straight to the family room. They (the jury) sat down on the couch, and I (the defendant) placed myself on the love seat.

For a few moments no one said a word.

When I couldn't stand the silence any longer, I aimed a tentative smile at my mother. "Did you enjoy Paris?" I asked.

"Very much. It was lovely."

"Oh, good. I'm glad you had fun."

It got quiet again and I fidgeted in my seat, wishing they'd just get to the closing argument already. I was aching to hear the verdict.

"Anya," said Dad at last, "we've been thinking an awful lot about what you told us."

"I kind of figured."

"We understand that this theater means the world to you," said Mom. "And we can only imagine how terrible you felt when you realized your clubhouse was off-limits."

They exchanged glances, as though trying to decide which one of them was going deliver the crummy news. Dad, it seemed, drew the short straw. He gave me a serious look.

"Anya, Mom and I have decided that—"

From the depths of my tote bag, my phone rang. Talk about bad timing.

I fished into the bag and checked the screen. "It's Susan," I said. "Should I get it? In case there's a problem?"

Dad nodded.

I swiped my index finger across the screen, then put the

call on speaker. "Hey, Susan. Everything okay?"

"I should be asking you that!"

Mom frowned.

I glared at the phone. "Kind of in the middle of something here, Susan. What's up?"

"Okay, well . . . Maxie wants to know if she should use the risers we found backstage for the extra Scylla heads to stand on, or if she should bring in milk crates or something."

I considered this. The last thing I needed was to have actors falling off wobbly milk crates on a dark stage. "I think for safety's sake, we should use the risers," I said. "They'll be sturdier. But send Maxie to the front desk and make sure she gets permission first."

"I'm on it. Thanks."

I disconnected the call, put the phone on the coffee table, and turned apologetic eyes to my parents. "Sorry. Go on."

Mom sighed and picked up where Dad had left off. "Lying is never acceptable, Anya. You know that, don't you?"

I was about to tell her I did know that, when my phone dinged again. This time it was a text message from Austin:

D wants to know if there's enough $ in the budget to rent a follow spot for the clubhouse.

"Austin has a financial question," I told my parents. "Do you mind if I . . . ?"

"Go ahead," said Mom.

"Okay. It'll just be a sec." I pulled my notepad and the budget report Susan had prepared for our business meeting with Matt out of my tote bag. I spread these across the coffee table and opened the calculator tool on my phone. I punched in a few figures, adding, subtracting. I compared the results to the paperwork, murmuring to myself as I did. "Hmm . . . okay, so adjusting for the cost of the stage weapons, and taking into account the Krause mini-mart ad . . ."

"Excuse me, did you just say 'the Krause mini-mart ad'?" asked Mom.

I nodded. "Uh-huh. We're selling advertising space in the program. Matt Witten has a professional arrangement with Mr. Krause, so I did a little networking and got him to place an ad for the filling station. He paid top dollar."

My father looked a little flabbergasted. "Ad space. Really."

"Matt Witten's going to promote his lawn service, and when we get a free moment, we're going to see if any more local businesses might want to jump on board."

"That's . . . very impressive," said Mom.

"Thanks." I made a few more calculations on my phone, then used the speech-to-text feature to respond to Austin. "Tell D I love the idea. We can probably swing it, but have him shop around and compare prices. Don't finalize anything until we discuss it."

I hit send, then turned back to my parents. "I'm really sorry about this. It's just that—"

My apology was cut off by the ringing of the house phone; we could hear Nana answering it in the kitchen.

"Wallach residence. . . . Yes, she is. Who may I say is calling?"

A moment later Nana appeared in the family room, holding the cordless phone. "Sorry to interrupt, dears. But it's a Mr. Jefferies. He says he's a reporter with the *Chappaqua Chronicle*, and he's asking to set up an interview with—and I quote—'Ms. Anya Wallach, the director.' "

Despite being in the middle of a sentencing hearing, I smiled. Mr. Jefferies had written an amazing article about our first show (thanks to Sophia Ciancio, believe it or not) and the fact that he wanted to do a follow-up interview with me about our second performance was kind of a big deal.

"Can I take the call?" I asked eagerly.

"Absolutely," said Mom. At the same time my father said, "Of course."

"Hi, Mr. Jefferies," I said in my most professional voice. "Thanks so much for calling. I'm in a meeting right now, but I'd love to set up a time to talk."

He gave me a few dates and times. I chose Tuesday

morning at the community center theater. This way, he could interview a few of the actors and crew members as well. I thought it would be way more interesting for the *Chronicle* readers to get input from other theater members, instead of just hearing about me.

I hung up the phone and once again turned my full attention to my parents. They were looking at me with the weirdest expressions on their faces. Neither said a word; they just looked from me to each other, shaking their heads and looking utterly amazed.

When I couldn't stand the suspense one minute longer, I blurted out the question I'd been stewing over for the last three days.

"Did you guys decide to make me cancel the play?" I asked.

Dad took a deep breath.

Mom looked down at her hands.

I gripped the sofa cushions for dear life and waited for an answer.

Finally my father looked me in the eyes.

"Yes," he said. "We did."

"Yes?" I echoed. My voice was a whisper. A croak. A gasp. It sounded exactly how I felt: as though every ounce of life had been drained out of me. "Yes, you decided to cancel the play?"

Mom nodded. "Yes, we did."

"Oh. Okay." I swallowed hard. "Well, I don't really blame you, I guess."

"Anya," said Dad, his face unreadable. "You have to understand. Mom and I talked about this for a long time and, ultimately, we came to the conclusion that making you cancel the play would be the right thing for us to do."

Yeah, I get it! I wanted to shout. *I heard it the first time; you don't have to rub it in!* Sniffling loudly, I kept my eyes low and managed a nod.

"But . . . ," said Mom.

But? I snapped my head up and saw that Dad was smiling. "We've changed our minds," he said. "Just now, in fact."

I looked at them in utter disbelief, as though, like Scylla the sea monster, they'd both suddenly grown five more heads.

"We had every intention of canceling your show," said Mom. "You broke the rules and you were dishonest. And for the record, you *will* be punished for that."

"Okay," I said, now at the edge of my seat. "But the show . . . What about the show?"

Dad shrugged, as though even he couldn't believe what he was about to say. "Anya, what you're doing here"—he gestured to my phone and the theater budget on the table—"is truly impressive. I can't imagine another twelve-year-old—or twenty-year-old, for that matter—handling a business with such natural ability. We saw how wonderful the first show was, but honestly, I don't think we really understood just how many behind-the-scenes responsibilities you had to juggle to bring it to life."

"I didn't either," I admitted. "Until they started happening."

"That's the point," said Mom. "You're stepping up and handling this like a real professional. All those other children are looking to you and counting on you to get the job done. And from where I sit, you're not letting them down."

Happy as I was to hear that, I felt a pang of guilt. "But I let you guys down," I said quietly. "And I'm so, so sorry."

"We know you are," said Dad. "And as Mom said, you're going to be punished for what you did. But canceling the show wouldn't just be punishing you, it would be punishing Susan and Austin and all the other members of the cast. That wouldn't be fair."

"I think the lesson here," said Mom, reaching over to take my hand, "is that sometimes in business you have to make hard choices. As an adult, I know bending the truth is never the right option, but we're taking into account that you're still learning. You're under a lot of pressure for someone your age, and in a moment of desperation you did what you thought was in the best interests of your business . . . even if not in the best interests of my washing machine."

I quickly pushed the spreadsheet toward her, pointing to a notation in red ink. "We've put aside some money to pay you back for the plumber's fee."

"Most important," said Dad, "you told the truth in the end."

He stood up just as my phone chirped again. A text from Maxie:

Jane refusing to wear crinoline! Way 2 itchy. Athena's wig tangled in lyre strings. Sophia demanding gold lamé toga. WHERE R U???

I showed my parents the message.

"Come on," said Dad, laughing. "We'd better get you back to that theater fast. Clearly, your cast needs you."

It was one of the best things "Ms. Anya Wallach, the director," had ever heard.

☆✿✿✩

A pretty cool thing happened during our second week of rehearsals. We really started to feel like part of the CCC community. Or maybe, more accurately, they started to feel like part of us.

Although we considered our rehearsals private, we never turned away any CCC employees who wanted to slip in and observe. Mrs. Crandall (who'd returned to her post at the swimming pool entrance) got into the habit of popping in during her lunch break to see how the show was coming along.

And it turned out that Mrs. McPhee, who'd taught Maddie and Jane's origami workshop, didn't just teach paper folding. She was a retired high-school art teacher who now worked part-time, overseeing all the arts and crafts activities that took place at the center. Her assistant, Kevin, was a summer volunteer who'd be heading off to the Rhode Island School of

Design in the fall to pursue a degree in fine arts.

On Monday, Kevin and Mrs. McPhee dropped by between workshops to offer Maxie and Brittany some cans of leftover paint to help complete our two enormous backdrops—one, a beautiful sunset over the Aegean Sea (which we'd use for all of Odysseus's wild adventure scenes), and the other an impressively detailed mural depicting the interior of his Ithaca home. In addition to this second backdrop, Gina had created two enormous Corinthian columns by stacking large cardboard cylinders (used for pouring cement pilings, and generously donated by her father) and spray-painting them grayish white. So Kevin taught Brittany a faux-painting technique called trompe l'oeil and assisted her in turning the cardboard pillars into stunningly realistic-looking architec-tural elements. Gina topped them off with ornately decorated capitals, which she'd created out of good, old-fashioned papier-mâché.

"Let's be sure to give Mancuso Construction a free plug in the advertising section of the program," I told Susan. "As a way of thanking Gina's dad for supplying the cardboard molds."

"Good idea." Susan made a note of it.

"And we should probably acknowledge Kevin and all the other CCC folks who've pitched in, too," I added.

"That's what I like about you," said my sister with a big smile. "You haven't forgotten about all the little people who've helped you make it to the top."

"Well, I'm not exactly there yet," I said, laughing. "And right now I'm not as worried about getting *to the top* as I am about getting back into the clubhouse theater."

But Susan was right. We had been fortunate to receive all kinds of help and encouragement from places we'd never even imagined, and I didn't want to miss the opportunity to let these benefactors know how sincerely grateful I was.

For example, when the day camp programs let out for the day, the counselors would give us all the leftover juice boxes and water bottles they hadn't distributed to their campers. And the front desk receptionist, Mrs. Sawicki, insisted on putting one of our posters in the lobby, as well as placing an announcement about the play in the CCC's weekly online newsletter.

On Tuesday, Mr. Jefferies came and conducted his interview. I told him all about why we had to move to the CCC. Then he spoke to Maxie about the challenges of costuming the play, and to Joey about switching from the guitar to the lyre. Sophia, of course, weaseled her way in and used the word *star* every chance she got. Teddy said something profound about how theater had helped him to grow as a person. Elle talked about how funny the song lyrics were.

By Wednesday everyone was off book (which meant they'd all memorized their lines and knew them by heart) and, for the most part, the dances were really coming along. Mackenzie's ballet solo as Calypso was absolutely breath-taking, and her jazz number during the big battle scene was a high-energy showstopper. Thanks to her, the suitors' tap dance was, in a word, hilarious. The swords had *still* not arrived, so for the time being we substituted these with pool noodles (thank you, Mrs. Crandall!).

Of course, it wasn't all sunshine and lollipops (and juice boxes). We had to deal with the rowdier day campers who were always listening at the door or trying to sneak in and spy on our rehearsals. And there were even a few CCC regulars who resented our temporary presence. I suppose on some level I understood that. If strangers ever started hanging around our clubhouse theater, I'd probably be pretty annoyed.

One girl in particular, who came every afternoon to use the computer room, was always giving me dirty looks. Her name was Tessa Trent; I knew because she had taken swimming lessons with me back in the day. Of course back then she wasn't a tough-as-nails rock 'n' roll wannabe.

On Thursday afternoon, Susan, Austin, and I were coming out of the theater into the main lobby. That was when we saw Tessa arriving, clutching her drumsticks. As always, she gave us an icy scowl.

"What's her problem?" Susan huffed.

I had been wondering the same thing all week, so I'd made a few inquiries. Now I told Susan and Austin what I had learned.

"According to Mrs. Sawicki," I said, "Tessa and some of her friends are in a heavy metal rock band."

"Well, that explains the eyebrow ring," said Austin dryly.

"They call themselves Upchuck," I went on.

"So gross," said Susan. "And yet . . . so fitting."

"Why is she always hanging around here?" asked Austin.

"She comes to use some really cool music-mixing software program they have on the computer," I explained.

"Then what's she got against us?" Susan persisted. "We don't go anywhere near the computer room."

I sighed. "Mrs. Sawicki told me that Upchuck was hoping to rent the stage for a week of band rehearsal and a concert. Tessa's even gone as far as appealing to Mrs. Napolitano to have us thrown out! She thinks since she's a full-time CCC member, she has more of a right to the auditorium than we do."

"It's not our fault we signed up for the theater before she

did," Susan observed.

"Odysseus had Poseidon," Austin quipped. "We've got her."

Tessa came stomping over in her lace-up boots. For one crazy second I thought she was going to start banging on my head with her drumsticks like I was a human snare drum.

"Aren't you done with that play yet?" she demanded.

"No," I said, trying not to sound terrified, and failing miserably, given the way she was glowering at me. "Not yet."

"Well, how much longer do you plan on hogging the theater?"

Unfortunately, I didn't have an answer to that question. Things were still very up in the air back at Random Farms, and I couldn't say for sure if we'd be needing the stage for that crucial third week of rehearsals (tech week!) and ultimately for the show. So I just smiled and said, "Excuse me, but my ride is waiting," then I grabbed Susan's hand and ran out of the lobby with Austin right behind us.

"She really wants us out," he observed when we were safely on the front steps of the CCC.

"I'm not worried," I said, remembering the day Mrs. Crandall had put us in the special events computer calendar. "We've got our pink highlight to protect us."

After that unpleasant encounter, it was a relief that

Friday's rehearsal went so well.

I arrived at the theater to find Maxie and Kevin, the arts and crafts volunteer, beaming over the sketches for Jane's Charybdis costume.

"It's a masterpiece," Kevin assured me on his way out. "You're going to love it."

I took a step toward Maxie, who quickly thrust the tear sheet behind her back.

"Wait!" she said, holding up her palm like a traffic cop. "The drawing doesn't do it justice. You have to wait until you can see the real thing."

"Okay," I said with a shrug. "So when do you think you'll be ready to unveil this masterpiece?"

"As soon as Jane gets here," Maxie promised. "You have to see this costume in action."

"I have to see a *costume* in *action*?"

Maxie gave me a nod and a smile. "You'll see," she said, her tone filled with mystery.

I would have pressed her for more info, but the rest of the cast had begun to arrive, and it seemed that everyone had a question for me.

Teddy (aka Odysseus) wanted to know if I could have Maxie somehow use makeup on his chest and arms to make his pectoral muscles and biceps look bigger and more defined. The term *airbrushing* was bandied about. I said if it was okay with Maxie, it was okay with me.

Sophia informed me that she was going to once again employ the services of her own personal hair stylist for the show. "But only for my role as Circe," she clarified. "Not Cyclops."

That made sense. I mean, really, Sophia's costume included a hood, and how much actual hair-styling can you do to a bath mat?

Brady had requested long white hair for his Poseidon scenes, which Maxie had been able to provide, thanks to the collection of weird wigs Mrs. Quandt had contributed. He tried it on for me, wondering if I thought it looked more godlike parted on the side or down the middle.

Some of the other actors had queries about lines and blocking. Nora wanted to know if I had any advice for crying on cue, and my Greek chorus, who were playing newscasters, suggested we find some handheld microphones for them to use as props.

"I'll have Brittany put them on the list," I said.

The only person who didn't approach me with urgent business to discuss was Mackenzie. She just breezed in with her dance bag—ten minutes late—and said nothing. I would have called her on her tardiness, but A) I didn't want to waste precious moments hearing her explanation, and B) I got the feeling something was up with her. Maybe her audition for the New York ballet company had gone badly. Or maybe she just really missed carbohydrates.

It wasn't until both Jane and Deon had arrived (because there was an important lighting cue involved) that we finally got our first look at the Charybdis costume.

And you'll just have to believe me when I tell you, it was definitely worth the wait!

✧✦✦

As the day rolled on, I became more and more anxious. To make matters worse, Sophia kept giving Nora dirty looks, and Mackenzie seemed distracted, constantly glancing at the clock.

"What time is it?" she asked just as I was about to give Travis a note.

"Time for you to get a watch!" I snapped. "And also time for you to stop worrying about what time it is and focus on rehearsal."

I felt bad for shouting, but I couldn't help it. I was a nervous wreck.

Travis looked at me kind of funny and asked, "Anya, are

you okay?"

"I'm just a little antsy," I confessed. "After all, today's the day I meet with Mr. Healy to find out if we can move the show back into the clubhouse theater."

"Yeah," said Deon, with a cautious look. "About that . . ."

Half the cast was suddenly looking as nervous and hopeful as I felt. And the other half looked downright disappointed. Deon, especially, looked like he had an opinion on the subject.

"D," I said. "What are you thinking?"

"I dunno," he said, shrugging. "I guess I'm thinking it feels like a step backward."

"What does?"

"Going back to that grubby old barn."

Those words stung. Had he really just called our theater a . . . a . . . I couldn't even bring myself to *think* the phrase!

"How can you say that?" cried Maddie. I was shocked to see her eyes welling with tears. "Don't you remember how hard we worked cleaning that place?"

"And our curtain," said Spencer. "Our curtain's pretty cool."

"But this place has great sound," Elle pointed out. "And look at these seats."

"And the lights are amazing," Sophia added.

This was no surprise. She was probably thinking about how gorgeous she was going to look playing Circe under the warm glow of the CCC's high-tech lighting effects.

"I *definitely* wanna go back to the clubhouse," said Gracie. "My brother complains every time he has to drive me here because it makes him late for work. He's making me do his chores around the house to make up for it."

"Two words," said Teddy, pointing to a vent near the auditorium ceiling. "*Air. Conditioning.*"

"Two more words," snarled Susan. "*Who. Cares?*"

I stood there, my mouth hanging open, as the entire cast began to bicker. Nora, Brady, Joey, Brittany, and Gina remained relatively neutral, since they had no preexisting ties to the clubhouse, but Joey did mention he couldn't imagine the acoustics at the old barn being anywhere near as good as they were here.

I turned to Austin. "You want to go back to the clubhouse, don't you?"

Austin bit his lip. "Well, you have to admit, this place is pretty outstanding."

I couldn't have felt worse if he'd kicked me in the shins. "Wow," I said, the disbelief clear in my voice. "Disloyal, much?"

"Oh, c'mon, Anya. Don't be like that. You know this

theater is incredible."

"It is incredible," I conceded, "but it's not ours. It was always supposed to be temporary. And I don't care how cushy the seats are or how high-tech the sound system is. That 'grubby old barn' was where we came together and did something fantastic. And we did it all on our own terms." I didn't realize I was yelling these words until I noticed the entire cast staring at me. Well, fine. They needed to hear it, too.

"Haven't you guys ever heard of loyalty?" I demanded. "Not to mention the fact that the clubhouse theater belongs to us and us alone. We're in charge. Doesn't that matter to any of you?"

No one answered. In fact, the room had gone completely silent. I could see them weighing what I'd said against the image of their friends and family taking in the show while reclining in those comfy seats, enjoying the cool air, and marveling at the clarity of the sound and the beauty of the light washes.

I imagined it too, and still, there was nothing I wanted more than to be back in our own theater.

"Maybe we should put it to a vote," Maxie suggested. "That seems fair."

It did. But that didn't mean I didn't hate the idea. "I don't know," I said stiffly. "I'm the producer and the director, and it's my job to make these kinds of decisions."

This reminder was met with blank stares, and a frown from Deon. As much as I wanted to stand my ground, I realized I'd probably be better off in the long run letting them have their say. So I swallowed hard and announced, "Fine. We'll vote. All those in favor of doing the show here at the CCC theater, raise your hands."

Sophia's hand shot up like a rocket. Then Deon's. Joey and Elle raised their hands very slowly . . . but they raised them.

I held my breath, waiting to see what Austin would do. . . . So far, he was doing nothing.

Then Brittany raised her hand (but I think her vote was based mostly on geography, since she lived only a few blocks from the CCC), and so did Mackenzie. Brady and Nora raised theirs, too.

Susan did a quick count. "Eight," she said, relieved. "Not a majority. We're going back to the clubhouse!"

The cast members who hadn't raised their hands cheered. I wanted to shout for joy, but I managed to contain myself. It wouldn't have been professional. Instead I addressed my comments to those who had voted for the CCC. "I'm sorry, guys. I know this place is terrific. But we're a kids' theater. And since this place is run by adults, not kids, I think we're doing the right thing by going back to the clubhouse." I smiled around at them. "No hard feelings?"

"Plenty of hard feelings," Sophia seethed. "But whatever. I still get an awesome solo, wherever we do the show."

Everyone who'd voted to stay at the CCC was frowning and rolling their eyes. Deon especially looked more than a little miffed. I told everyone to take a three-minute water break. Then I approached Deon.

"D?"

"What?"

"You've gotta understand—" I began, but he cut me off with a cold look.

"Why do I 'gotta' understand, when you don't?" He shook his head and I could tell he was more frustrated than angry. "You didn't even listen to me, Anya."

"Yes, I did."

"No, you didn't. What I was saying made a lot of sense. But all you cared about was being in charge and not answering to grown-ups."

I considered this. He wasn't entirely without a point. "Fine," I said. "That's a little bit true. But don't you like how it feels not to have to answer to anyone?"

"I wouldn't know how it feels," he said in a clipped tone. "Because *I* answer to *you*."

With that, he stormed off to the control booth.

"That didn't go well," said Austin, approaching me and wearing a grim look.

"You wanted to stay here too, didn't you?" I said. "But you didn't raise your hand."

"Doesn't matter," he said. "It still wouldn't have been a majority."

"But it would have made it a tie. Then we would have had to figure it out some other way, and it might have ended with us doing the show here."

"Well, it didn't."

He wasn't being snotty, just matter-of-fact. I sighed. "So why *didn't* you vote to have the show here?" I pressed.

"Because as much as I care about lights and sound and really good acoustics, I care about you more."

I blinked. Had I heard him correctly? Did he just say he cared about me?

"As a director," he added quickly, as if he'd read my mind. "I care about your directorial vision. And as a colleague, too." He gave me an awkward shrug. "If going back to the clubhouse theater will make you happy, then it'll make me happy too."

It was the best answer he could have given me.

☆⭐☆

I could barely focus during the last half hour of rehearsal. We were running the opening dance to "Gotta See a Man About a Horse," and it just wasn't coming together as well as anyone would have liked. I think it had something to do with the fact that the kids who'd lost the vote were still upset. And besides that, we'd put so much effort into the suitors' big tap-dance-slash-sword-fight number, we hadn't allowed ourselves much time to perfect this one. The basics were all there, but there was still a lot more fight choreography that needed to be added, interspersed between the dance steps.

And still no weapons. My actors were doing a great job of miming in time to the battle sound effects on the CD. But I really wanted those phony spears and swords for the performance! Especially since we'd paid for them in advance. Right now, though, the bigger problem was the "Horse" number itself.

"The show goes up in a week, people," said Austin from his place at the electronic keyboard. "We've got to figure out a way to make this work. Let's try it again."

The dancers grumbled but returned to their starting positions and did it again. Better, but still not flawless.

I wanted to contribute, but I was so nervous about meeting Mr. Healy that no matter how hard I tried to concentrate, the entire number was a blur.

Mackenzie raised her hand. "Austin, Anya . . . I kind of have to go."

"Now?" I asked, checking the time on my phone. "But there's still another twenty-five minutes left of rehearsal. And you're the dance captain."

"I know," said Mackenzie, her tone a mix of guilt and apology. "But I've kind of got somewhere to be, and I can't be late." She turned to Becky. "Do you think you can finish tweaking the choreography without me?"

Becky considered it. "I guess I could. I mean, I can add the combat stuff, but I really don't know much about dance other than what I've been learning from you. I'm not sure I'll be able to come up with the right steps on my own."

"Kenz," said Susan, "the 'Horse' dance is one of the biggest numbers in the show. Are you sure you can't stick around a little longer?"

I wasn't sure if it was Kenzie's sense of responsibility or the fact that this request had come from Zeus that did the trick, but after a moment of what was clearly some difficult deliberation on her part, Mackenzie nodded.

"Okay," she said. "Dancers, from the top . . ."

Deon hit the CD play button, and the sounds of crashing shields and whizzing arrows filled the auditorium. Over these came Teddy's voice, singing:

Beware of Greeks with gifts, they say.
But that's our plan to save the day.
To topple Troy, we'll fight full force,
But first we gotta see a man about a horse.

Mackenzie counted out the steps, and Becky shouted reminders like, "Parry! Thrust! Duck!"

I watched until I couldn't stand the suspense a moment longer—I needed to talk to Mr. Healy now or I might actually explode. Confident that my dancers were in good hands, I told Austin and Susan to meet me at the clubhouse as soon as they could. Seconds later I was sprinting through the lobby, offering a quick smile to the receptionist as I headed for the door.

"Anya . . . ," she called after me. "Wait . . . I have a message for you."

I knew it was rude, but I pretended not to hear. I dashed out the door without so much as a backward glance and galloped down the front steps to where Mom's SUV was idling at the curb.

Because whatever the receptionist's message was, it couldn't possibly be more important than getting to the clubhouse to meet Mr. Healy.

✩✮✩✩

Mom dropped me off at the end of the street because there were still a number of road workers and city trucks, as well as a police cruiser, blocking the clubhouse driveway.

I waved to the workmen as I hurried past.

Stepping back into the shadowy clubhouse theater, I understood exactly how Odysseus must have felt when his sandals finally hit the gravelly shores of Ithaca and he was able to enter the castle he'd longed to see for so many years.

I felt as if I were coming home.

Home. Even without the Christmas lights shining or the folding chairs arranged in their orderly rows or the piano music rippling through the air, the clubhouse theater still felt as familiar and welcoming as it always had.

I immediately became aware of a deep, muffled growling sound coming from somewhere down below. Immersed as I'd been in Greek mythology for the last two weeks, my first thought was that there was either some great hulking beast prowling around our basement, or Poseidon had sent a combination earthquake-hurricane-tidal wave to completely ruin my day.

But of course, neither of these were the case.

Chapter Seventeen

"Mr. Healy?" I called out into the vibrating hum.

"Be right with you," came his voice from backstage.

A moment later he appeared, sweeping aside our custom-made **RANDOM FARMS KIDS' THEATER** curtain. Frowning, he strode to center stage as if he were about to perform some tragic Shakespearean soliloquy.

In that moment I had my answer. I felt the tears spring to my eyes, but I fought them back.

"I'm sorry, kid." Mr. Healy said this in his usual gruff voice, but I could hear the sympathy beneath his words. "The structure's still sound, which is good, but that rumble you're hearing is a couple of giant industrial fans. We're using 'em to dry out the basement. Gotta get rid of every last trace of moisture, ya see, or we run the risk of growing toxic mold. Public Works is afraid it's still too damp to turn the power back on, which is why we've got the fans running on a portable generator."

"Oh, all right," was all I could say.

For a long moment Mr. Healy and I just stood there, staring at each other. I think maybe I was waiting for him to say he'd made a mistake, that what he'd really meant to tell me was that the clubhouse was perfectly safe and ready for our immediate occupancy.

But of course, he didn't say that.

So I let out a long breath and said, "Thanks anyway, Mr. Healy."

I was about to leave when I remembered I hadn't kept my promise about asking if Matt could cut the back lawn. And although I wasn't really in the mood to seal any business deals at the moment, a promise was a promise.

So I explained Matt's proposition to Mr. Healy. He thought about it for a moment, then nodded. "Might as well let the kid give it a good once-over. Nothing fancy, though—we don't need any flower beds or perennial borders or anything like that back there. I'd just like him to cut the grass and clear out the weeds. I'll pay him his going rate. Tell him he can start tomorrow."

"I will, Mr. Healy," I said glumly.

Then I turned and walked out of my theater. My heart ached, and my stomach roiled.

But at least my eyes (unlike the clubhouse basement) were dry.

CHAPTER

Susan and Austin were just arriving on their bikes when I stepped out of the dimness of the theater and onto the front lawn of the clubhouse.

"Well?" said Susan, letting her bike fall to the grass. "What did he say?"

"Can we come back?" Austin prompted.

All I could do was shake my head and keep walking. I wasn't sure where I was going exactly; I guess I was just too filled with emotions crashing around inside me to make myself stand still.

Susan ran to catch up and threw her arms around me. "Anya, that stinks. I'm so sorry!"

"So am I," I said, wriggling out of her hug and doubling my pace. She and Austin fell into step beside me.

"Are you okay?" Austin asked.

"Sure," I said, the word falling from my lips like a dull, unpolished stone. "Why wouldn't I be? The show will go on."

I continued my hearty stride around the corner of the clubhouse and didn't stop until I'd come to the vast, sloping meadow that stretched out behind the barn, that tangle of weeds and overgrown grass that, tomorrow, would face the wrath of Matt Witten's ride-on mower.

And that was when I screamed.

It was a sound of pure frustration—a bellow, in fact. A shout of sheer and utter disappointment.

Susan and Austin looked on with wide eyes as the shrillness of my voice echoed down the rocky hill, over the field, and into the brilliant blue of the sky.

"Wow," said Susan. "The acoustics out here are amazing."

Surprisingly, as soon as I finished the scream I felt a whole lot better. For a while we just stood quietly, looking out over the field. The lumber that had been carried out of the basement still sat there in the high grass, dry now from two weeks in the summer sun. I wondered what Mr. Healy was going to do with it. Put it back in the basement, most likely, once the place dried out.

"Listen, Anya," said Austin at last. "Maybe it's not exactly what we wanted, but let's face it: the community center theater isn't such a bad place to put on a show."

"I know."

"And just think, we won't have to spend all that extra time setting up the chairs," Susan pointed out.

"That's true," I allowed. "I guess it won't be so bad. It's just . . ." I trailed off with a sigh.

"I know what you mean," said Austin, glancing toward the clubhouse. Even from out here we could still hear the deep whirring of those powerful fans. "It's like that scene in the play when the god Aeolus gives Odysseus a giant bag of wind as a gift, and he tells him that he's not supposed to open it until he's home. They almost make it, too, but just when they're close enough that Ithaca's coastline is in sight, one of his men opens the bag against Odysseus's orders, and the wind escapes, causing a raging storm that blows them back out to sea. Odysseus has to start his journey all over again." He paused to shake his head. "It's kind of a bummer. He was so close. . . ."

"So close," I repeated softly, following Austin's gaze to the clubhouse.

Susan's phone made the twinkling sound that indicated she'd just received an e-mail. She tapped the screen a few times, then read silently. "Uh-oh. This isn't good."

"What now?" asked Austin.

"It's an e-mail from the stage weapon people."

211

"Finally!" I said. "Where are our swords?"

Susan gave me a worried look. "Well, according to this . . . they're still in the factory warehouse. In China."

"China!" I squawked. "That's not possible. We ordered them days ago. They should have shipped already."

"Yeah, it says that, but . . ." Susan consulted the e-mail, shaking her head in disbelief. "Oh, you are not going to believe this."

"Try me," I said.

"Okay, well, the sword people are very sorry to inform us that they will be forced to reimburse us for our order because . . ."

Her voice faded into the rumbling din of the fans churning in the basement.

"Susan . . . ," I urged. "Come on. . . . Because why?"

"Because their entire fleet of cargo planes has been grounded for the last several days due to . . . *high winds.*"

For a moment I just gaped at her. High winds? First floods, now high winds?

"Anya . . . ?"

I must have had a very strange expression on my face because Susan was suddenly looking very concerned. "Are you all right?"

My answer was a giggle.

And then the giggle turned into a chuckle. The next thing I knew, I was laughing so hard, the tears I'd been holding back since Mr. Healy had given me his grim report were now streaming down my face. I was laughing so hard, I was crying. Because if you really stopped to think about it, the whole thing was actually, kind of, almost, sort of completely and totally . . . *funny*!

Ridiculous. Ironic. And ROTFL funny!

So I laughed. And then Susan and Austin started laughing, too.

Because honestly, at this point, what else could we do?

✩✦✧✩

On Saturday, Susan, Austin, and I went on an ad-selling spree in town.

I was happy to find that many of the business owners who'd so kindly allowed us to put up posters in their windows were just as happy to purchase ad space in our program. This was a good thing because, even with the money we'd be reimbursed for the undeliverable stage weapons, renting the theater for a third week was going to take a pretty big bite out of our budget.

We'd just finished selling a half-page ad to the manager

of the coffee shop when my phone chirped. It was a text message from the CCC receptionist.

LARGE PACKAGE JUST ARRIVED AT FRONT DESK FOR RANDOM FARMS KIDS' THEATER. PLEASE COME PICK IT UP AT YOUR EARLIEST CONVENIENCE.

"Maybe they were able to ship the stage weapons after all," cried Susan, taking an enthusiastic bite into the cupcake she'd charmed the barista into giving her for free.

It was as good a guess as any. Maybe the gods had decided to smile on us after all. We headed straight to the CCC.

When we got to the community center lobby, the receptionist handed us a large cardboard box. We tore into it, hoping to see an entire arsenal of swords, spears, and clubs.

But it wasn't the stage weapons.

It was Deon's portable follow spot. The one he'd rented when we were still holding out hope we'd be having the play in the clubhouse. Now that we'd be performing in the state-of-the-art CCC theater, with its high-tech lighting board and sound system, we had no use for the portable spotlight.

"Should we send it back?" Susan asked.

"Might as well," said Austin. "I'll have Deon bring it to the post office on Monday."

"I hope the rental fee is refundable," I grumbled, although

the way my luck had been running, I doubted very much that it would be.

Suddenly Susan's face went pale.

"What's wrong?" I asked.

"Upchuck!" she whispered.

"You're going to be sick?" I asked. "Do you need me to take you to the bathroom?"

"No," said Susan, pointing across the lobby. "Upchuck. The band."

I whirled to see Tessa Trent strutting across the lobby, grasping her omnipresent drumsticks. But this time three more girls were with her. One carried an electric guitar hanging from a shoulder strap.

A terrible feeling began to wash over me as my eyes went from the spotlight box to Tessa's band—who, I realized, was heading directly for the theater entrance!

"Mrs. Sawicki," I said, panic rising in my throat. "Why did you call me down to pick up this spotlight? Why didn't you just wait and give it to me on Monday morning?"

Mrs. Sawicki looked confused. "Because I didn't expect to see you on Monday. According to Ms. Napolitano, your rental agreement expired at the close of business yesterday. I called out to you when you were leaving. I wanted to say good-bye and wish you luck with the show, wherever you ended up holding it, but I guess you didn't hear me. You seemed like you were in a hurry."

"Please . . . ," I said, my voice rasping. "Please tell me the theater hasn't been rented for next week."

"I'm sorry, dear, but it has," she said, pointing to Upchuck. "Tessa and her band start rehearsing first thing Monday morning. In fact, they're setting up for it now."

"I don't understand," said Austin. "I thought we reserved the theater for next week."

"You put it on hold," Mrs. Sawicki corrected. "Which meant you had until the end of business yesterday to make your payment. You didn't, so the hold became null and void. Since you hadn't contacted Ms. Napolitano to extend your rental agreement, we just assumed you'd gotten your old venue back."

I closed my eyes and saw a computerized calendar with a band of pink highlight disappearing from next week's dates.

I'd forgotten to renew the rental.

And now the theater had been reserved right out from under us for a week's worth of heavy metal madness!

"Hey!"

I opened my eyes and saw Tessa smirking at us from the theater doorway. "You guys better get your theater junk out of here. We need to set up our instruments."

Chapter Eighteen

Austin quickly took out his phone and called Gracie while Susan used hers to call Mr. Healy in the neighborhood association's maintenance office. I assumed they were requesting the use of Nick's pizza car and the groundskeeper's pickup truck to haul our belongings out of the theater and deliver them to . . .

To . . .

That was the problem: *To where?*

CHAPTER

"We have to cancel the play."

"We aren't going to cancel the play."

"Austin, c'mon. . . ." I was seated beside him in Nick's pizza delivery car. The trunk was packed with all the things we'd hastily collected under the scathing glare of Tessa Trent and her fellow Upchuckians. Mr. Healy's pickup was right behind us, with Susan in his passenger's seat and the bulkier set pieces (like our two gorgeous backdrops, neatly folded) secured in the bed of the truck.

Of course, we had nowhere to hang them now.

"What about having the play in your backyard?" Gracie suggested from the front seat (over the blare of Nick's voice advertising that night's pizza special over the car's PA speakers). "Wasn't that the original plan when you started the theater?"

"It was," I said. "But there's no way that's happening now."

I gave a glossed-over version of how I'd blatantly abused my parents' trust. "Anyway, this production needs a much bigger space." I thought of the dance numbers and the clanking of our nonexistent swords. "Not to mention great acoustics."

Great acoustics . . . where had I heard that before?

"So that's it?" said Austin. "You're giving up?"

"What choice do I have?" I shot back. "It's not like Athena is going to send Hermes down to point me in the direction of the nearest theatrical venue."

As I said it, I saw something through the car window that just might well have been the most inspiring sight I'd ever seen in my life.

Not Hermes.

Matt Witten. On his father's ride-on lawn mower!

Heading toward the clubhouse.

"Nick, stop the car!"

Nick swayed the car toward the curb and hit the brakes.

"What's going on?" asked Austin. "Anya, what are you thinking?"

"I'm thinking that everything we know about theater today originated in the outdoor amphitheaters of ancient Greece." I gave him a big smile. "At least, that's what I've heard."

It took a minute for him to understand what I was suggesting.

Then he practically dove out of the car, and we were racing after Matt.

✫✫✫✫

Getting permission to hold our show outdoors on the clubhouse property was much easier than it had been to get the go-ahead to do it inside. I still had to consult with the Neighborhood Association president, Dr. Ciancio, but this time things went much, much differently.

Austin, Susan, and I knocked on the Ciancios' door, all dirty and sweaty after unloading the car and the pickup truck and lugging all our theater belongings into the clubhouse for safekeeping.

Sophia opened the door and made a face. "You guys are a mess."

"We know," I said. "Sophia, there's been a change of plans."

As she stood in the open doorway and listened, I gave her the SparkNotes version of the situation, from the temporary hold I'd placed on the CCC theater, to a girl with an eyebrow ring, to my realization that the clubhouse back lawn bore an uncanny resemblance to an ancient Greek amphitheater.

"Technically, the lawn is a neighborhood common area," I concluded, "so we need to ask your dad if he'll sign off on letting us do the show outside."

I felt my sister and my theater partner beside me, holding their breaths. I was sure they were remembering, like I was, the horrible deal we'd had to strike with Sophia the first time we found ourselves in this unenviable position.

But to our collective shock, Sophia simply turned and called through the foyer, "Daddy! We're doing our play on the clubhouse back lawn."

Dr. Ciancio's voice floated back to us from deep inside the house where (I couldn't help but imagine) he was probably busy polishing Sophia's solid gold toothbrush or perhaps grooming her brand-new pony.

"Whatever you say, princess," was his immediate response.

"Wow," said Susan. "That was easy. While you're at it, do ya think you can get him to purchase a full-page ad in the program?"

"Consider it done," said Sophia.

With that, she slammed the door in our faces.

"Susan, text everyone," I said. "Let them know we're having an emergency meeting tomorrow at the clubhouse." I gave her a smile. "Tell them we're coming home."

THE RANDOM FARMS KIDS' THEATER
PRESENTS
THE ODD-YSSEY
AN EPICALLY FUNNY MUSICAL
To Be Performed
Under the Stars
Time and Date TBA via Social Media
In Our New Outdoor Amphitheater
On the Back Lawn of the Clubhouse Theater
BYO Blankets and Lawn Chairs

Sunday was a whirlwind of reorganization.

Susan's text brought everyone to our new venue bright and early, with the exception of Brady, who was at his grandfather's birthday party somewhere in New Jersey, and Maddie, who had to go to her cousin's bridal shower in Ossining.

Tried to get out of it, Maddie texted. **But I'm the junior bridesmaid, so my attendance is sort of mandatory.**

Mackenzie was also a no-show. This had me furious!

I considered calling her on the Fleisches' house line, but with everything I had spinning in my brain at the moment, the last thing I wanted was to have another awkward phone conversation with Mrs. Fleisch.

The first thing we did was check the extended weather forecast. I had Deon consult his weather app.

"The week should be clear and sunny for rehearsals," D reported. "Except for a passing thunderstorm on Tuesday morning. Should blow through by lunchtime, though. And for the record, this wouldn't be an issue at an indoor theater."

I gave him a look.

"What about the weekend?" asked Austin.

It came as no surprise to me (and I was sure it wouldn't have shocked Odysseus, either) that the weekend called for heavy rain, beginning Saturday afternoon and going into late Sunday night.

"How's Friday look?" asked Teddy.

"Gorgeous," said Deon.

"Friday it is, then," I pronounced. "Opening night. We lose a whole day of rehearsal, but we'll just have to deal. And we're gonna have to push our start time to a little later in the evening. I'm thinking the curtain shouldn't go up until nine o'clock. I know it's late to be starting but we need to wait for full dark."

Joey turned a teasing eye to Travis, Elle, and Gracie. "Can you fifth graders stay up that late?" he joked.

"Yes, we can," said Elle. "And for the record, we're not fifth graders anymore. We're about to be sixth graders."

"And besides," Travis added, "I'm Athena. So I operate on goddess time."

"That's great for you, Trav," I said, "but since the rest of us are mere mortals who operate on regular old Eastern Daylight Time, we'd better get to work."

And so we did.

Matt had done a fabulous job of cleaning up the meadow and the sloping hillside. He promised to come back on Friday morning and do it again so the area would be perfectly trimmed and manicured for the show.

Which would be taking place on a brand-new, custom-made outdoor stage!

Because the night before, I had arranged a meeting with Gina and her dad, Mr. Mancuso. I'd told him about the bind we were in, and that although we could not pay him to help us build a stage, we'd be more than willing to barter for his services.

"What did you have in mind?" he'd asked, sipping his espresso.

I'd glanced at Gina, who'd sat across from me at the Mancusos' kitchen table, engrossed in the blueprints she'd been drawing. "Gina tells me her grandparents live in a retirement community over in Mount Kisco."

"They do," Mr. Mancuso had confirmed.

"She told me they have an awesome common room, with a stage and everything. And sometimes singing groups or dance troupes come to entertain the people who live there."

"That's right."

"I was thinking that in exchange for you and your construction crew building us an outdoor stage, maybe Random Farms could visit your parents' place and put on a show for the residents . . . free of charge."

Gina had looked up from her work and smiled at her father. "Nona and Pop would love that," she'd said. "Don't you think?"

Mr. Mancuso had smiled. "I'm sure they would," he'd said. Then he'd extended his hand to me and we'd shaken on the deal.

So today Mr. Mancuso had sent a crew of builders with hammers and saws and a whole arsenal of power tools over to our clubhouse. Using the blueprints Gina had drawn up, and the reclaimed lumber from the basement, they set to work building us a sturdy, low-lying stage platform. Behind that, they constructed a tall, broad frame from which we could hang our backdrops. Thanks to some ropes and pulleys, we would be able to interchange the backgrounds by rolling up the Aegean scene like an enormous window shade and revealing the painting of Odysseus's house behind it.

The gentle slope of the hill would act as our seating section. Thanks to a fair amount of jutting stones and boulders (which, according to Austin, were able to trap and reflect sound), our audience would be able to hear us clearly without microphones, just as the lines spoken by the legendary actor Thespis and his buddies had been heard and enjoyed by Grecian theater patrons thousands of years before.

"There's not a bad seat in the house," Austin remarked happily as we stood at the top of the stony slope and looked down to where our cast would perform *The Odd-yssey* in less than a week. "The voices are going to carry beautifully."

"And Deon's spotlight is going to work perfectly!"

General lighting had at first presented a bit of a snag, but Mancuso Construction owned several large portable lights that the company used for outdoor night jobs. The lights would be there in time for dress rehearsal. I was thrilled to learn these were all battery-powered, just like D's spotlight. The fog machine, for our scenes on Mount Olympus, however, was not.

"And the electronic keyboard does run on batteries," Austin explained, "but even if we put in brand-new ones on the night of the show, I'd still feel a lot better if we had a backup power source."

So we were going to require electricity.

Also not a problem. Mr. Healy deemed that two nights without fans would hardly result in an outbreak of toxic mold, so there was no reason why we couldn't borrow the portable generator . . . and the giant fans as well. Using the fans was Gina's idea; she pointed out that we could use them to blow supercharged gusts of breeze, providing incredibly realistic winds to enhance Odysseus's daring scenes at sea!

"And the strobe feature on my spot could be lightning," said D.

Two of Becky's brothers, Charlie and Ben, came toting two oversize camping tents, which they set up behind the stage.

"Dressing rooms," said Becky. "One for boys, one for girls."

I pronounced her the world's smartest combat choreographer.

And as far as stage combat was concerned, I wasn't even upset that we'd be performing our battle scenes without any actual weapons. My cast was by now so accomplished at miming their swordplay, it had become an art form in itself—an exercise in imagination for both the actors and the audience—with the invisible blades swinging and clashing in perfect sync with the sound effects.

The sound effects! Even these were getting special attention. They would be amplified into the balmy night in all their whooshing and clinking glory courtesy of Nick Demetrius and the pizza car's loudspeaker. This was another idea I had and was able to execute, thanks to the barter system. I remembered how Nick had used the speaker to get Gracie to hurry up after rehearsal, and I realized it was just another version of a microphone. We "purchased" the use of Nick's vehicle's loudspeaker under the following arrangement, which I dreamed up and then had approved by Gracie's uncle George, who owned the pizza place. Austin, Susan, and I would volunteer to hand-wash the pizza car once a week for the rest of the summer.

When the sun began to fade into a velvety lilac twilight, Austin and I finally sent everyone (including Mr. Mancuso's building crew!) home.

"I think we're going to be all right," said Austin, getting on his bike. "I think Odysseus would be proud of us."

"It'll make a great story someday," I conceded. "The epically funny tale of how Random Farms put on its second show."

"Quit complaining," said Susan, heading for home. "We've got an amphitheater. How many twelve-year-olds can say they've got their own amphitheater?"

Chapter Nineteen

She was right. None of it was how we had planned it, but I realized that was what made theater such a rush. The inevitable disasters and the subsequent fixes were why being a producer was so exciting and challenging.

What I didn't know at the time, though, was that our biggest challenge was still ahead.

CHAPTER

On Monday, as Susan and I walked to the clubhouse, I phoned Mrs. Sawicki and asked her for a favor.

"Of course I'll run the new announcement in the online newsletter," she said in her pleasant way. "And please hold two tickets for me at your will call window. I wouldn't miss this show for the world!"

"Thanks," I said. "Your tickets will be waiting for you. Compliments of the house."

Susan frowned. "We don't comp."

"We do now," I told her.

In addition to the CCC newsletter, Susan tweeted the information so our cast could retweet and let all their friends and families know about the switch from Saturday at seven at the community center to Friday at nine on the clubhouse back lawn. We also printed flyers announcing the change of date, time, and venue.

Knowing how much pressure we were under, Mom offered to drive into town and post the flyers in all the store windows where we'd originally placed our posters. This was a huge help, since I couldn't spare a single cast or crew member.

Susan and I arrived at the clubhouse to find everyone present and accounted for.

Everyone except Mackenzie.

"She's probably just running late," said Susan.

"Again," I said, feeling a knot of anger in the pit of my stomach. "I'll stand in for her."

We ran the show, with me as Mackenzie's temporary understudy. This took longer than usual, since every time I needed to make a note, I had to stop the action.

I shouted out lighting cues, which Deon jotted down. Unfortunately, we wouldn't get to actually rehearse with our donated lights until Thursday. Same went for the fans. Which reminded me . . .

"Maxie, make sure you put everyone's wigs on extra tight. That wind factor is going to make a big difference. And the last thing we want is a bald Athena."

"Speaking of wind," said Sophia, "I've been thinking that I'd like to add some kind of long flowing cape to my costume. It'll look great blowing and billowing in the breeze during my 'Men Are Pigs' solo." She strutted to the costume area and chose a filmy drape of fabric from Maxie's costume collection. "Hmmm. This will do nicely."

"But that's Penelope's cape," said Maxie.

"Not anymore," trilled Sophia, swirling the transparent cape around her.

"That's not fair," Nora protested. "Maxie designed that for me."

"Too bad," Sophia said in an icy tone. "First Circe took your man, now she's taking your accessories."

"Oh, no she's not," said Nora through her teeth, reaching for the hem of the cape and attempting to jerk it out of Sophia's grasp. "And for the record, Odysseus went back to Penelope."

"Let go!" Sophia demanded, tugging the fabric.

"You let go!" Nora shouted, pulling harder.

"I'm wearing it!" *Tug.*

"Not if I can help it." *Pull.*

Riiiippp.

The next thing I knew, each girl was clutching half a cape. A collective gasp rose up from the cast as we all stared in shock at the tattered fabric.

"Wow," muttered Teddy. "I'm sure glad they weren't fighting over Odysseus."

To their credit, both actresses looked terribly guilty as they handed the pieces of ripped cape to Maxie.

"I think I can fix it," said Maxie with a sigh.

"Good," I said curtly, frowning at Sophia and Nora. "And when you do, I'm letting Athena wear it."

Neither Circe nor Penelope gave me an argument.

With the exception of the cape catastrophe and Mackenzie's glaring absence, the rest of rehearsal went really well, which made me feel better. We got in the habit of taking SPF breaks every two hours so everyone could reapply their sunscreen.

"I bet this isn't something real Broadway directors have to contend with," I joked to Austin.

On Tuesday, as predicted, we were delayed by the thunderstorm. (I triple-checked with Gina to make sure she'd put the painted backdrops inside the clubhouse the night before.) The waiting made me a little anxious, as I wanted every possible minute of rehearsal time we could get. But I told myself we could all use a little rest. And it was the perfect time for me to find out what in the world was going on with Mackenzie.

So I put on my rain jacket and Wellington boots, grabbed Dad's giant golf umbrella, and ran the two blocks to the Fleisches' house.

When Mackenzie answered the door and saw it was me, her face crumbled.

"Kenz, what's the deal?" I asked tersely.

"I was going to text you later," Mackenzie said, her eyes darting away from mine. "I . . . um . . . well, I'm not going to be able to do the play."

As I stared at her, my eyes round with shock, a loud clap of thunder shook the Fleisches' front porch. "You're kidding, right? Please tell me you're kidding."

"I'm really sorry, Anya."

"But why?" I asked, my tone softening at the sight of her trembling lower lip. "Did you pull a muscle? Are you sick or something? I don't understand. Why can't you be in the play?"

"I just can't." Mackenzie shook her head, her eyes shining with tears. "I wish I could but I can't. Please tell everyone I said break a leg." She paused, then added, "And good-bye."

"Kenz—"

But the door had already closed in my face.

CHAPTER

By lunch the storm clouds had cleared—out of the sky, at least. I felt as if my heart were filled with them. In any case, I arrived at the amphitheater under a brilliant blue sky. Deon, Gina, and Brittany were hanging the backdrops while Austin set up the electronic keyboard.

"I've got some bad news," I told the cast. "Kenzie's out."

"Out?" Elle repeated. "What do you mean by 'out'?"

"She can't be in the play."

"Why?" asked Spencer. "She was doing so great as Greek Chorus Number One."

I shrugged. "I don't know exactly why. She just said she couldn't be in the play. Maybe it has something to do with the change of date from Saturday to Friday. Maybe she's got a big audition or something."

"Will she be back for the next show?" asked Nora.

"Of course she'll be back," was my answer. But in truth, it was really just a guess, based not so much on Mackenzie having actually said she would, but on the fact that she hadn't said she wouldn't.

"This is a bit of a problem," said Austin. "She's Calypso, and she's got that major dance number during the fight scene. And all the coolest battle moves depend on her. Not to mention all her newscaster lines."

"I'm not too worried about the chorus part," I said. "We can divide up her lines between the other newscasters. You guys all know her part, right?"

The actors who switched in and out of chorus roles nodded.

"Good," I said. "That's solved. Maddie, I'm putting you in the role of Calypso. Can you learn the lines?"

"Sure," said Maddie. "But I'll never be able to do those ballet moves."

I thought for a moment. "Well, Calypso doesn't have to be a ballerina. You're a cheerleader, right?"

Maddie nodded.

"So maybe you can goddessize some of your cheer dance moves for Calypso."

Maddie's eyes lit up. "I can so totally do that."

Then I took a deep breath and turned to Becky. "Now

236

all we need is someone who can fill in for Kenzie during the battle scene."

"What?" Becky looked terror stricken. "Anya, no. No way. Are you crazy?"

"It's a challenge," I said. "But, Bex, you know the combat choreography better than anyone. And I'm sure after all those extra fight calls and rehearsals, you must have picked up Mackenzie's dance steps. You guys worked so closely on mixing the dancing into the sword fighting."

Becky bit her lip. "Well, sure . . . I *know* the steps. I just don't think I could ever do them as well as Mackenzie did."

"We're not asking you to do them as well as she did," I said evenly. "We're just asking you to do them as well as you can. And don't sell yourself short. You can be really graceful when you want to be."

"But you're asking me to do this in front of people," said Becky. "I'm not a performer."

Susan laughed. "Excuse me, but you are totally a performer. You play sports in front of crowds all the time. You do backflips off the high dive in front of a panel of judges!"

"Please, Becky," I said. "We really need you."

It took about three seconds for my lifelong BFF to say she'd do it.

"All right then," I said, in my best directorial voice. "Time to get to work."

☆☆☆☆

On Wednesday morning we did a complete run-through without stopping once. It was fabulous. The songs sounded terrific, the scenes were hilarious and exciting, and the dances were spot-on. Becky may not have had the elegant ballerina style Mackenzie brought to the performance, but she more than made up for it with her easy athletic poise and fluidity.

The afternoon was devoted to our cue-to-cue rehearsal (not easy since the majority of our lights and pizza car wouldn't be available until Thursday afternoon) and our final costume fittings.

Sophia made a terrifying Cyclops and a stunning Circe.

"Talk about range," Susan observed. "She can pull off being a monster and a goddess."

"Susan," I said, blinking at my sister in wonderment. "You just said something nice about Sophia Ciancio!"

"I know," she said with a sigh. "I guess playing the father of the gods has made me a little more understanding of you poor flawed humans."

Before we knew it, Thursday had arrived. Dress rehearsal!

We'd be running the play from start to finish in full costume and makeup, using all of our (admittedly limited) tech.

Since we wouldn't be able to get a true sense of how our lighting worked until after sundown, we decided to hold off on dress rehearsal until dusk.

That left me with the whole day to sit around and obsess about things like Brady's long white wig blowing off his head in the middle of his song, or Nick getting called away to deliver some emergency pizza order in the middle of broadcasting our all-important battle sound effects, or whether Maxie would remember to bring enough safety pins to attach the curly little tails to the soldiers' backsides after Circe turns them into pigs.

Or . . .

My stress was interrupted by a text from Becky.

HOW ABOUT A SWIM?

I smiled. It was a great idea. So I texted back:

SOUNDS GOOD. R U ALREADY AT THE POOL?

My best friend replied:

YEP. MADDIE, GRACIE, AND JANE JUST WALKED IN TOO. BRING SUSAN.

I texted back:

BE RIGHT THERE.

I went upstairs to notify Susan and change into my

bathing suit. *Nothing like a little socializing at the town pool to calm a producer's nerves*, I thought.

But I was wrong about that. Because when we arrived at the pool half an hour later, I found myself more nervous than ever.

Not because of the play.

But because Matt Witten was standing at the end of the diving board.

And he was smiling at *me*!

☆✦☆✦

It was a moment before I realized Matt was no longer on the diving board. He'd executed a flawless front flip and was now swimming toward the ladder.

A giggle and a nudge from Susan got my feet moving toward the lounge chairs where not only Gracie, Maddie, and Jane were sitting, but also Spencer and Travis. Sophia was letting Elle French-braid her hair (seated as far as possible from Nora, who was flipping through a magazine), and Teddy was a little ways down on the pool deck, showing off his Hacky Sack skills to Deon, who didn't even wave when I arrived.

I tried not to let that bother me. But it did.

Chapter Twenty-One

"Brady and Austin just went to the snack bar for sodas," Jane reported.

I beamed. "Looks like everybody had the same idea," I said, tugging off my T-shirt and shorts and smearing sunscreen on my cheeks and nose.

"The gods on Olympus used to do this sort of thing all the time," said Susan knowingly. "Random get-togethers, just to celebrate their own awesome godliness. Of course, there was usually a lot of ambrosia flowing at those shindigs." Her eyes shot to the concession stand. "Maybe I can get someone to spring for an ice-cold Dr Pepper."

She skipped off toward the snack bar, where I was sure she'd be able to con Austin into buying her a soda. Over the last several weeks, they'd become pretty good pals. I think for Susan, Austin was like the big brother she'd always wanted.

"Anya!"

I looked up to see Becky climbing out of the pool and then dripping her way across the concrete deck, a huge smile on her face.

"Okay, so . . . it wasn't actually *my* idea to text you," she confessed.

"It wasn't?"

"Well, I mean, of course, I would have wanted you to come and hang out, but I thought you'd be all wrapped up in play stuff for tonight, and I didn't think I should bother you."

She was grinning so broadly that I found myself smiling, too. "Then why did you?" I asked. "Not that it's a bother."

Becky leaned in to whisper the reason in my ear.

"Because Matt asked me to!" she said.

"Seriously?"

Becky nodded.

"Matt Witten came up to you and said, 'Text Anya and tell her to come to the pool'?"

Becky nodded again. She was smiling so hard, I thought her cheeks might explode.

"OMG."

Becky laughed. "He really likes you, Anya."

"Well . . . what do I do?" I asked, hoping everyone would mistake the deep-red blush of my cheeks for rapid-onset sunburn. "Should I wave? Should I go talk to him?"

"I don't think you have to," Becky said. This was because Matt was now heading in our direction.

I immediately wondered if my hair looked okay.

"Hi, Anya."

"Hi, Matt."

In the next heartbeat, Austin was standing beside me as though he'd materialized out of thin air. Susan was hot on his heels. And she was holding a bottle of Sprite.

"They were all out of Dr Pepper," she explained, her eyes locking on Matt Witten.

"Wasn't sure you'd be here," said Matt, smiling right at me. "I figured you'd be busy getting ready for the show."

"Nope," I said. "Not busy at all."

"Anya's not the type to stress out," Becky informed him. She knew as well as I did this was a flat-out lie. In fact, I was stressing out big-time right now. . . . *Was there a glob of unsmeared sunscreen on my nose? Should I have worn a nicer swimsuit?*

"I was thinking," said Matt. "Since I am an advertiser, I should probably see the show." He shook some water out of his hair. "Not that that's the only reason. I mean, I would wanna see it anyway."

"Well, I'll be happy to comp you a ticket," I said.

Susan frowned. "Again with the comps?"

I ignored her and went right on smiling at Matt.

Who was still smiling at me.

And then . . . it happened!

"So, Anya . . . ," he said, sounding a little nervous. "I was wondering, would you maybe want to . . . I dunno . . . like, hang out Saturday night or something? We can go to the arcade. Or bowling or something?"

It took me a second to register that I had just been asked

out on a date.

A date! I, Anya Wallach, had just been asked out.

On a *date*!

The reason I knew it was really happening was because I heard my sister actually gasp in absolute shock.

Without even thinking, I said, "That sounds fun, Matt. Sure. I'd love to."

I only hoped he couldn't tell my knees had begun to quiver. This was my first official date request, after all.

"Great," said Matt. He sounded a little relieved, as if he hadn't been entirely positive I would accept.

Then Susan, ever the helpful little sister, gave me a nudge to the ribs. "Anya . . . I hate to be the one to break it to you, but you are *so* not allowed to date!"

I had a sudden image of myself pouring her entire soda down her throat just to shut her up!

"Oh," I said grimly. "That's actually a good point."

"Well, it won't be a date if we all go."

This very astute observation had come from Austin. I turned to him, looking confused.

"What are you talking about?"

"What if we all go?" he said with a shrug. "You and Matt, and me and Becky."

"Technically, that's a double date, Romeo," Susan pointed

out wryly. "But I bet you've got a way better shot at getting Mom and Dad to okay that, as opposed to just you and Mr. Brown Eyes here canoodling on your own."

Matt laughed. Apparently, he (like everybody else on the planet) found Susan adorable. "Sounds like a plan," he said. "Becky, you in?"

Did he really have to ask? It was pretty obvious from the way she and Austin were suddenly grinning at each other like a couple of goofballs, Becky was all for it.

Now all I had to do was get Mom and Dad's permission.

✩✮✩✩

"A date?" my father said. "As in . . . a *date*?"

We were standing in the foyer. The front door was still open behind him, since I was approaching him with this request the minute he walked in from work. I had dragged Mom to the foyer with me because I knew this was the kind of request they would have to process as a team.

I nodded. "Yes. A date as in a date."

Dad's eyes narrowed, his forehead furrowed. "You're asking if you can go on a date?"

"A double date," I clarified quickly. "Becky and Austin are going, too. And it's not the kind of date you guys used to go on back in the olden days."

"Oh," said Mom, grinning. "So then this young man *won't* be coming to pick you up in his Conestoga wagon?"

"You know what I mean. We're just going bowling. Lots of girls my age go bowling with groups of friends. Some of them even go to the movies, which is way more date-ish than the bowling alley."

My parents looked at each other, conferring silently.

"Who is this boy?" my father asked.

"Matt Witten."

"The kid who cuts the lawn?"

"He prefers the term *arborist*," I said.

"And he's got some seriously gorgeous brown eyes," Susan added, poking her head in from the family room. "Just sayin.' "

Another look passed between Mom and Dad.

"All right," Mom said at last. "You can go. But this will be a daytime activity, and we'll be dropping you off and picking you up. Tell your date he can meet you at the alleys at eleven o'clock."

I totally could live with that. I flung my arms around her and hugged. "Thank you!" I cried.

An outdoor play and a double date at the bowling alley! Something told me this was going to go down in history as one of the best weekends of my life.

Chapter Twenty-One

That evening, as the stars began to twinkle over our amphitheater, we had our dress rehearsal.

Any actor or director would tell you there was just something about "dress" that was both thrilling and nerve-wracking. It wasn't quite the show, but it was more than just a rehearsal. It was the culmination of long weeks of preparation and exhausting work.

It was your last chance to get it right.

Your show—your precious show—that had been once just a script and some songs, was now a living, breathing thing. And you knew in your heart that even if a thousand different companies were to perform it a thousand different times, it would never look or sound or *be* exactly the same as your show. Every play was the result of some unique and magical alignment of talents, personalities, and events, all coming together (or, in some cases, falling apart) to be something utterly original.

But for me, the truly poignant thing about dress rehearsal was this: it was the very last time your play belonged to just *you*. On opening night, you would give it away. That was what a performance was, after all. . . . It was you giving your show to the audience, offering it, like a gift, to these people who'd come to enjoy it. You would kiss it good-bye and send it out into the world, with all its perfect moments and silly mistakes.

Dress rehearsal was the last time you and your cast could say this was ours . . . because tomorrow it would be *theirs*, too. To enjoy and to remember. And you could only hope the audience would love it every bit as much as you did.

"Anya?"

I snapped myself out of these thoughts to see Austin looking at me expectantly. "Ready?"

I wasn't, not really. I wanted to keep this play to ourselves just one second longer. But that was not what a director did. So I nodded.

"Bon voyage, Odysseus," I whispered to the sky. Then I took a deep breath and smiled at my cast. "Places, everyone!" I called.

It was time to begin.

☆❀☆☆

As dress rehearsals go, this one was pretty tame. We had a few forgotten lines and some costume delays, and there were some technical issues to work through.

Getting the wind effects right, for example, was tricky. On

the high setting, the fans made the backdrops whip and flap so ferociously, it looked as if the Aegean were in the throes of a monsoon. "Try low," I suggested to Deon. It worked.

The actors spoke clearly and loudly, and the acoustics were totally in our favor. Austin positioned himself at the top of the slope and swore he could hear the actors' every word. Even the ones they got wrong!

For example, in the scene where the Greek chorus (known in the script as the Eyewitness Muse Team) reports that Aeolus, the god of wind, has given Odysseus a bag of breeze, Gracie got tongue-tied and said *Aioli* had given our hero *a bag of fleas.*

"Bet that would have really 'bugged' Odysseus," Susan quipped. "And who is Aioli? The god of mayonnaise?"

Poor Elle! She played the swift-flying Hermes with a huge amount of heart and energy, but she just could not seem to nail the weird pronunciation of Calypso's island.

"O-guy-guy-yay?"

"No," I told her patiently. "Oh-jee-jee-yuh."

She tried again. "O-giggy-goy-ah?"

"Closer." Then I said it again more slowly. "Oh. Jee. Jee. Yuh."

Elle nodded and repeated after me: "Oh-jee-jee-yuh."

"Yessss!" cried Austin, running down the slope to give her a high five. "Perfect."

Sadly, our six-headed Scylla monster needed a bit of rethinking. Since we no longer had the CCC's risers to work with, we settled for lining up the five additional actors behind Spencer and having them poke their heads out one at a time. It wound up being pretty hilarious, but deep down I'd really wanted to create the illusion of disembodied faces floating around.

"Maybe next time," Maxie said.

It was close to ten thirty by the time we were ready to rehearse the curtain call.

"Sorry, there's still no theme song," said Austin.

Believe it or not, I had almost forgotten about it, what with all the other issues that had come up. "It's okay," I told him. "We've been busy."

"I promise," he said, "we'll have it for the next show."

"The next show," I repeated, smiling. "Okay."

Because this time I had no doubt in my mind there would be a next show. Random Farms was in business for the long haul now. And there was nothing that could stop us.

There was only one way to say it: *The Odd-yssey* was a complete triumph, a full-on crowd pleaser, and an enormously huge success.

(Okay, so maybe there were three ways to say it.)

From the moment Teddy walked onstage and sang his opening number, "Everything Is Epic," we knew we had a hit on our hands.

Brady and Susan got roars of laughter when surfer boy Poseidon complained to Zeus that Odysseus had "O-dissed him big-time, dude." And Sophia was by turns terrifying and hilarious as Cyclops.

"Maxie, you did a great job with that costume," I whispered while we watched from backstage.

"Never underestimate the power of a well-tailored bath mat!" Maxie replied.

The best undisputed laugh line of the night wasn't actually from the script at all; it was an ad lib from Elle (as Hermes), who shouted to Odysseus as his ship left Calypso's island:

"Oh-jee-jee-yuh . . . wouldn't wanna be ya!"

If we'd actually had aisles, the audience would have been rolling in them.

All in all, our production wound up being a combination of moments so right and perfect, they surprised even us. But there were also plenty of silly goofs and unlucky pitfalls of the sort that have actors silently reminding themselves the show must go on.

Our "perfect moments" went as follows:

The lights Gina's father's electrician set up for us were great, and Deon's rented follow spot worked like a dream.

The clashing of swords and spears booming through the pizza car's speaker created a truly chilling effect as the sounds echoed into the darkening night. And the fact that there were no actual weapons gave the battles a weird and eerie quality.

"Let's hear it for pantomime," said Susan.

Nobody missed a single line of dialogue, and the comic timing was flawless.

Nora cried on cue. Athena was amazing. And the Cyclops scared us all half to death.

It was the costumes that really blew me away, though.

The togas looked awesome, and even the pigs looked professional, but the undisputed wardrobe highlight was Jane's Charybdis costume—a work of artistic genius and incomparable creativity! Maxie had taken an old Hula-Hoop and draped it with jagged strips of sheer blue fabric and green tulle of varying widths and lengths, and embellished these shreds of material with glittering sequins and crystals. Deon used one of the colored gels that came with the portable spotlight to shine a circle of aqua-blue shimmer on her, and when Jane set the hoop in motion, the fabric fanned out and fluttered, spinning and twinkling. She really did look like a furiously churning whirlpool.

The only noticeable mistake (that totally had us cracking up) was a scenery glitch; Gina and Brittany forgot to roll down the sunset backdrop and left the interior of Odysseus's house in place for the Siren scene. It looked as if our hero's ship was sailing through his living room.

When the cast finally came out to take their bows, the crowd rose from their blankets and lawn chairs and applauded wildly.

We'd done it again.

"It was an adventure," said Austin, giving my shoulder a congratulatory squeeze. "But in the end, the theater gods smiled on us."

I turned to Deon, a huge smile on my face. "See, D?" I said. "Even without the lights and the microphones, it all turned out great, didn't it? And now that we know we can rent portable lights and stuff, maybe next time when we're back in the clubhouse theater we can—"

Deon cut me off with a shake of his head. "You might have to find another tech guy for next time, Anya. One who doesn't mind that his opinions don't matter."

My mouth dropped open. "What?"

"D, what are you saying?" asked Austin.

"I'm saying I'm not sure if I'll be back for the next Random Farms performance."

Onstage, the cast had their arms outstretched to acknowledge the stage crew. With a shrug, Deon jogged out to join Maxie, Brittany, and Gina for their bows.

"What just happened?" I asked Austin, my eyes wide, my heart racing. "Did he just . . . quit?"

Austin frowned. "I think he's just still upset about the vote. Give him some time to cool down and think it over. He'll be back."

"Are you sure?"

Austin's answer wasn't exactly an answer. "Let's enjoy the moment," he said. "After all, if there's one thing we learned from this odd odyssey, it's that there's no telling what the gods have in store."

I managed a smile and shifted my focus from Deon's shocking words to the joyful sound of cheers and applause. It had been an exciting journey, with all sorts of challenges, and what I'd learned was that while heroes and battles might be thrilling, when you got right down to it, friendship was the most epic adventure of all.

As I watched my cast take one final bow, I knew Austin was right: the theater gods *were* smiling on Random Farms.

And I didn't want to miss a second of it.

☆ ☆ ☆

I woke up Saturday morning feeling proud and a little sad. I loved that the show had been a success. But I hated that it was over.

When I went downstairs, I found Susan already at the kitchen table, counting our ticket money.

"We made a fortune," she informed me. "In case you were wondering."

One look at the amount of cash and I knew she wasn't exaggerating. Between the box office earnings, our advertising revenue, and our bake sale income (minus the cost of the CCC theater rental, the follow spot, and a few other various expenses), we were left with what Susan called "some serious bank."

When my dad came down to breakfast, I took a ten-dollar bill from the table and met him at the coffee maker.

"Here," I said handing him the cash.

He looked perplexed. "What's this for?"

"It's . . . um . . . well, what's it called when someone hires you to be their attorney?"

"A retainer."

"Okay," I said, smiling. "That's what this is . . . a retainer. Random Farms is hiring you to be our lawyer."

"I'm flattered," said Dad, opening the bag of coffee and scooping some into the machine. "But why in the world do you need a lawyer?"

"Yeah," said Susan, squinting at me. "Why in the world do we need a lawyer?"

"Because we used all those songs and scenes in *Random Acts of Broadway* without paying the licensing fees, that's why."

"Oh, that," said Susan, pushing aside the piles of money and reaching for the Cheerios. "I forgot about that."

"Well, I haven't," I said firmly. "Dad, we need to settle up with all the people or companies who own the rights to everything we used in our first show. I'm not sure exactly how we do that yet. . . . I guess I'll have to research who owns the rights, then write letters or send e-mails explaining that when we used the material, we didn't know about permissions and licensing fees. Now that we do know, we want to do the honorable thing and pay what we owe."

My dad was staring at me with a weird expression.

"What's wrong?" I asked. "Is ten dollars not enough to secure your legal services?"

"It's not that," said Dad. "I guess I'm just a little thrown off by your bringing this to my attention after the fact."

"I think what Dad's trying to say," said Susan, pouring some cereal into a bowl, "is that you already got away with it, so why bother?"

"I'm not saying that at all," my father said. "I'm saying that I feel like maybe I dropped the ball a little by not advising you on this issue for the first play."

"But you didn't even know what songs we were using until you saw the show," I pointed out. "So how could you have known we were using them illegally?"

"That's true," Dad allowed. "And in my defense, intellectual property isn't my area of expertise. Honestly, it just never occurred to me that there would be a problem."

"Aw, don't beat yourself up about it, Dad," said Susan, munching on her Cheerios. "We didn't realize it either until we tried to license *Annie*. But we've got the funds to settle up now, so it's all good."

Dad tucked the ten dollars into the pocket of his bathrobe and smiled. "Consider me officially on retainer and, if I may say, officially proud. Not only about this, but for the incredible job you did on *The Odd-yssey*. It was a fantastic show. I loved the way you chose to mime the battle scenes. It was very imaginative and unusual."

"And unavoidable," muttered Susan.

I was helping myself to a bowl of cereal when the doorbell rang.

"Can someone get that?" called Mom from upstairs.

"I will!" I replied, breezing into the foyer. I suspected it would be Becky, or maybe Austin showing up with the morning edition of the *Chappaqua Chronicle*. With any luck, there'd be an excellent review of our show in the arts and entertainment section.

But when I opened the front door, it wasn't Becky or Austin.

It was Mackenzie. And her mother.

And there was nothing excellent about that.

"What do you mean, you quit?" I heard myself saying.

I wasn't sure how I'd managed to get the words out, what with Mrs. Fleisch scowling at me like she was. From the second I'd opened the door, she'd been looking at me as if I'd done something truly awful and unforgivable. It was kind of a miracle I'd even heard Mackenzie say what she'd said.

Which was, *I'm quitting the theater.*

"I don't want to quit," Mackenzie said, her voice trembling. "I have to. My mother's making me."

"But why?" I was careful to address this to Kenzie and not her glowering mother.

"Because . . . I lied. I lied about being part of the theater right from the start. I pretended to go to the dance studio because I knew my mother would never let me join Random Farms if I told her the truth. I really thought I could pull it off, and even if I couldn't, I convinced myself it would be better to beg for forgiveness than to ask for permission."

From the look on Mrs. Fleisch's face, I had a feeling the forgiveness part wasn't going quite the way Mackenzie had hoped it would.

"Can you imagine my shock, Anya," said Mrs. Fleisch, "when I went to pick up Mackenzie from dance class on Friday afternoon and she wasn't waiting for me outside as usual? I was a nervous wreck! I went inside and her dance teacher explained that she'd been missing classes for weeks!"

So that was why Mackenzie had wanted to leave early on Friday. To get to the studio before her mother did. I'd made her stay late . . . and she'd gotten caught. Not that I thought it was okay for her to be lying to her mother. But I hated being the reason she was in trouble. The whole thing was a mess!

"Do you know how important Mackenzie's dancing is to her?" Mrs. Fleisch asked.

"I do," I said. Then I mustered up my courage and, in as respectful a tone as I could manage, I said, "But maybe the theater is important to her, too."

At this, Mrs. Fleisch sighed. "Anya, what you've put together here is very admirable but it's not a professional theater."

That assessment hit me like a slap across the face.

"I disagree," I said. "We've all worked very hard. We put on a terrific revue. And last night's show was a huge hit. We got another standing ovation, and we made twice as much money as we'd even hoped for."

"I'm happy things went well last night," Mackenzie said, her expression earnest. "But I think you're going to have to use some of that money to hire a choreographer for future shows."

"Future shows?" Mrs. Fleisch shook her head and patted my arm as though she actually thought she was being helpful. "I'm sorry to have to be the one to tell you this, Anya, but I doubt very much there are going to be any 'future shows.'" She turned and started down the porch steps. "Let's go, Mackenzie. You have a lot of classes to make up."

"I'll be right there," said Mackenzie.

Frowning, Mrs. Fleisch hesitated, then continued on her way, leaving us alone on the porch.

"What did she mean there aren't going to be any future shows?" I asked, struggling to keep the anger out of my voice. "Kenz, has your mom done something to put an end to the theater?"

"No," Mackenzie said quickly. "She hasn't done anything, but I heard her talking on the phone to some of the other moms."

"Saying what?"

Mackenzie was wringing her hands. "Saying school starts in two weeks, and that I'm hardly the only kid who has extra-curricular commitments."

She had a point. I thought of Sam's baseball responsibilities, and Joey's guitar lessons. Maddie and Jane would have cheer practice starting in September, and I was pretty sure Travis and Spencer both played in the youth football league.

"Well, we can be flexible," I said. "We can work around those things."

"I hope so," said Mackenzie. "But I heard my mother tell Mrs. O'Day that she doubts very much many parents will allow their children to skip their professionally taught lessons and activities to take part in a twelve-year-old's backyard theater." She paused. "I think Mrs. O'Day agreed with her. So did Mrs. Walinski."

At the curb, Mrs. Fleisch gave a quick blast on the car horn.

"I'm really sorry, Anya," said Mackenzie, tears welling up in her eyes. "I just wanted to give you . . . ya know . . . a heads-up about this. If the other moms decide not to let their kids be part of Random Farms, well . . ." She trailed off, finishing with a shrug. Kenzie gave me a hug, then hurried down the steps.

All I could do was stand there, watching her go, my mouth hanging open and my mind spinning.

It was true that when I'd first come up with the idea for the theater, I'd imagined it as a summer activity. But somewhere along the way it had become much bigger than that. It had to keep going! We'd found a theater of our own, we had a reliable business model, and most important, we had a group of talented actors, dancers, and singers who shared a love of theater and a willingness to work hard.

For crying out loud, we even had an attorney on retainer!

But I suddenly found myself wondering if any of that would matter when school started and all those tempting sign-up sheets and permission slips for teams and clubs and organizations began to circulate. Activities run by grown-ups, who handled all the details and headaches so the kids could just show up and have fun instead of worrying where the follow spots and costumes and set pieces were coming from.

And what about homework? Tests, projects, and book reports . . .

Would my cast and crew be able to handle all that and rehearsals, too? And there was still the question of whether Deon would come back, not to mention the fact that Sophia and Nora could barely stand the sight of each other!

So what did all this mean for the future of the Random

Farms Kids' Theater?

I really and truly did not know.

Only after Mrs. Fleisch's car had sped away did I notice Austin jogging across the front lawn. He was carrying the morning *Chronicle* and smiling his head off.

"The reviews are in," he announced, waving the newspaper over his head like a flag. "The headline reads, and I quote, 'They've Done It Again! Random Farms Has Stunning Success with Second Show.' "

"That's great," I said, forcing myself to return his smile.

He frowned at me, noticing that I was still in my pajamas and bathrobe. "Hey, did you forget about the big double date? Shouldn't you be dressed already?"

"Oh. Yeah. Right." But I had forgotten about it. I'd forgotten all about Matt and Becky and bowling and everything else in the world. "Just give me a minute," I said.

☆✩☆✩☆

As I trudged up the stairs, I tried to let the excitement of the fact that I was about to go on my first real date push all the miserable thoughts about what Mrs. Fleisch had said out of my brain.

After all, I was going bowling with a cute, smart guy, and

my two best friends were joining us. I had everything to be happy about.

Didn't I?

In my room, I changed into the shorts and shirt I had picked out to wear today. It was the perfect outfit. I could picture Becky at this very minute, rifling past all the soccer jerseys and running pants in her closet to get to that adorable cotton skirt with the scalloped hem she loved so much but rarely wore. This made me smile.

Our first double date.

I picked up my hairbrush and gave my long dark hair a few strokes. Susan and I had debated for a full hour before we went to bed last night about how I should wear it. We'd decided on a messy bun, that all-purpose casual style that made me look closer to thirteen and a half than just plain twelve.

When my hair was done, I smeared on a bit of tinted lip gloss and felt my spirits begin to lighten.

Because, really, I had an awful lot to be happy about. I had great friends and an awesome family, and I was pretty sure Matt liked me as more than a friend, which was a totally new and flattering experience.

And over the last few weeks I had (with a whole bunch of help and support) succeeded in putting on two amazing shows. I was seriously proud of that, and I'd always be proud of it.

Even if two turned out to be the limit.

Even if we never got to do another show as Random Farms.

Which I desperately hoped would not be the case. But right now it was hard to say what was going to happen.

"Hey."

I turned to see my sister grinning in the doorway. "Hey."

"You look great! Matt's going to be swept off his feet."

I blushed. "Thanks, Susan." Then, on an impulse, I ran to her, threw my arms around her, and hugged her as tightly as I could. "Thanks for everything."

"Uh . . . oh-*kay*. You're welcome?" The baffled look on her face made me laugh.

As I picked up my purse and slung it over my shoulder, Susan cocked her head and asked, "So what was all that about with Mackenzie before? Did I hear Mrs. Fleisch talking to you? Sounded pretty intense."

"It was," I admitted. "But I'm not going to think about it right now."

With that, I gave Susan a brave smile and headed down the stairs.

LISA FIEDLER

Lisa Fiedler is a lifelong fan of musical theater. She saw her first Broadway play at age seven and has been badly belting out show tunes ever since! Her books for children and young adults include the Mouseheart trilogy; *Romeo's Ex: Rosaline's Story*; and *Dating Hamlet: Ophelia's Story*. She and her family divide their time between their home in Connecticut and their cottage on the Rhode Island seashore.

ANYA WALLACH

Anya Wallach is the real-life creator of the Random Farms Kids' Theater, a not-for-profit organization she started in her parents' basement when she was a teenager. Today the Random Farms Kids can be regularly seen on Broadway and in film and television. Anya also created the theater's extensive outreach program, with a focus on bullying prevention. In conjunction with Random Farms, Anya has been featured in the *New York Times* and on Fox News and *Teen Kids News*, and was recognized by the *Huffington Post* for her work as a young social entrepreneur. She lives in New York City, where she runs Random Farms full-time. Learn more at www.anyawallach.com and www.randomfarms.com.